"Film Props, Inc., is a two-acre attic in West
Hollywood stuffed with moose heads, spectacles, armor, space suits, and the lab equipment of half the
mad scientists in movie history. Rummaging for props
to rent, I once found a gun belt marked 'Mr. Wayne'
and a parlor lamp marked 'Tara.' That's as close to the
big time as I ever get.

"I'm a film director. Oh yes, and the guy who
sprays lane markers on a freeway is a painter.

"Well to be honest, I've done a few commercials . . ."

Meet Stoney Winston . . .

DOUBLE EXPOSURE
A Hollywood Mystery

Bantam Books offers the finest in classic and modern American murder mysteries. Ask your bookseller for the books you have missed.

Stuart Palmer
The Penguin Pool Murder
The Puzzle of the Happy Hooligan
The Puzzle of the Red Stallion
The Puzzle of the Silver Persian
Murder on the Blackboard

Craig Rice
The Lucky Stiff

Rex Stout
Broken Vase
Death of a Dude
Death Times Three
Fer-de-Lance
The Final Deduction
Gambit
The Rubber Band

Max Allan Collins
The Dark City

William Kienzle
The Rosary Murders

Joseph Louis
Madelaine
The Trouble with Stephanie

M.J. Adamson
Not til a Hot January
A February Face
Remember March

Conrad Haynes
Bishop's Gambit, Declined
Perpetual Check

Barbara Paul
First Gravedigger
The Fourth Wall
Kill Fee
The Renewable Virgin
But He Was Already Dead When
   I Got There

P. M. Carlson
Murder Unrenovated
Rehearsal for Murder

Margaret Maron
The Right Jack

Ross Macdonald
The Goodbye Look
Sleeping Beauty
The Name Is Archer
The Drowning Pool
The Underground Man

William Murray
When the Fat Man Sings

Robert Goldsborough
Murder in E Minor
Death on Deadline

Sue Grafton
"A" Is for Alibi
"B" Is for Burglar
"C" Is for Corpse

R. D. Brown
Hazzard
Villa Head

A. E. Maxwell
Just Another Day in Paradise
The Frog and the Scorpion

Rob Kantner
Back-Door Man
The Harder They Hit

Joseph Telushkin
The Unorthodox Murder of
   Rabbi Wahl

Richard Hilary
Snake in the Grasses
Pieces of Cream

Carolyn G. Hart
Design for Murder
Death on Demand

Lia Matera
Where Lawyers Fear to Tread
A Radical Departure

Robert Crais
The Monkey's Raincoat

Keith Peterson
The Trapdoor

Jim Stinson

DOUBLE EXPOSURE

Jim Stinson

BANTAM BOOKS
TORONTO · NEW YORK · LONDON · SYDNEY · AUCKLAND

This edition contains the complete text
of the original hardcover edition.
NOT ONE WORD HAS BEEN OMITTED.

DOUBLE EXPOSURE

A Bantam Book / published by arrangement with
Charles Scribner's Sons

PRINTING HISTORY
Scribner's edition published November 1985
Bantam edition / April 1988

ISBN 0-553-26665-9

Published simultaneously in the United States and Canada

Bantam Books are published by Bantam Books, a division of Bantam
Doubleday Dell Publishing Group, Inc. Its trademark, consisting of the
words "Bantam Books" and the portrayal of a rooster, is Registered in
U.S. Patent and Trademark Office and in other countries. Marca Regis-
trada. Bantam Books, 666 Fifth Avenue, New York, New York 10103.

PRINTED IN THE UNITED STATES OF AMERICA

KR   0 9 8 7 6 5 4 3 2 1

For Emer—and for Sue

DOUBLE EXPOSURE

Candy had used him. "Then she went to work for some Bible-thumper in Burbank, for about six months — until the

1

FILM PROPS INCORPORATED IS A TWO-ACRE ATTIC IN WEST Hollywood stuffed with moose heads, spectacles, armor, space suits, and the lab equipment of half the mad scientists in movie history. Rummaging for props to rent, I once found a gun belt marked "Mr. Wayne" and a parlor lamp labeled "Tara." That's as close to the big time as I ever get: fondling saintly relics of my faith—finger bones and hanks of hair from movies long since canonized.

Today, I'd collected two surfboards and a volleyball set for Harry Hummel's cola commercials ("Kids at the beach, okay? Lotsa tits and teeth") when ancient Merv behind the counter called me to the phone. I walked through this sanctuary with honest reverence, threading past rubber swords, plowshares, plastic Tikis, and a flyblown gorilla, toward the front of the musty building.

The call was from Hummel: "Winston, get your ass over here."

"Harry, you won't believe this: I found a surfboard from *Gidget Goes Hawaiian*."

"What?"

"I'd love to use it, but the design's too dated."

"What? What is this? Will you get your ass over here?"

"You said that."

Click.

I sheathed the surfboards in the hatch of my ancient yellow Rabbit (1975 was not a vintage year for Volkswagen), flagged their protruding sterns to mollify the law, and struggled east on Santa Monica Boulevard toward Finart Studios, the ramshackle production lot on which Hummel rents an office.

As I rattled through the smog, the next few days un-
reeled before me, predictable as death: out to Malibu
Beach with two trucks, a generator, and station wagons full
of "talent" and wardrobe. Two days playing film director in
sand-filled shoes, the sun broiling my dismaying new bald
spot into a dime-sized plate of scrambled eggs. Two days
more in my editor hat, faking the footage into some kind of
sense. Then three weeks of unemployment while hustling
another job.

Dear Mama: I am in Hollywood. It is fun. I am a big
director now. You were wrong.

Oh yes: scrambling at the grubby edges of the Industry, presiding over cheap local commercials and droning in-
dustrials, writing training films to keep afloat and feature
scripts for agents to reject.

I paused at the studio gate, to find One-Arm Willard
snoozing as usual in the gatekeeper's booth.

"Willard!"

His sleeping finger stabbed reflexively at a button and
the gate lifted to admit me. Riffraff come and go unchecked
while Willard slumbers on.

I should have stuck with acting. I'd be just as poor and
pointless and just as much a whore, but at least I could work
a nice warm brothel, instead of ankling around the streets.

I chugged along the tarmac road dividing scabby bungalow offices from soundstages that resembled stucco hang-
ars. The Rabbit wheezed to a grateful halt in a parking
space marked HARRY HUMMEL LIMITED. The perfect
adjective for my employer.

Hummel was lurking in his scruffy office, behind a
midden of crumpled production forms and take-out food
wrappers that hid a grandiose pre-war mogul's desk, now
rapidly shedding its oak veneer.

As always, he skipped the pleasantries: "You line up
the location, Winston?"

"How about Coronado for a change?"

"How many times do I have to tell you: no more than
thirty miles from the goddam gate."

"I love your finesse with adjectives, Harry."

"What?" He struggled with that briefly, then reached the limit of his attention span and shrugged. Harry Hummel's forty-four, with brass-blond hair and pale ceramic eyes. In the beard he's forever starting, he resembles Henry VIII, just growing fat.

I sighed. "Malibu again?"

"Whatever." He waved it off. Hummel stared at me, tried to invent a transition, failed of course, and plunged in anyway: "Do something for me."

I returned his stare.

"Look at this tape."

He pushed a videocassette into a Beta recorder on the swaybacked table behind his desk and clicked on the color monitor. The speaker whispered electric hash and the screen displayed a snazzy pattern reminiscent of Hummel's taste in sport jackets.

Aping bigger producers, he'd bought the rig to tape auditions, product tests, locations. But being Hummel, he'd spent three weeks locked in his office with a stack of porno tapes and then tired of his toy.

Sure enough, the picture coming up was the same sad ritual of clenching buns and straining faces and of course the ancient piston and cylinder: the wet machine. It must have been a so-called "loop," a crude, silent effort without even a pretense of story. A carnal documentary of the crassest kind.

Hummel stared sourly at the tiny, striving figures. "I know the girl. That's Lee Tolman."

I didn't bother to look. "One of your ladies, Harry?"

He killed the tape irritably. "I didn't say I screwed the kid—just knew her."

"Why the past tense?"

"Huh?"

Give me patience. Slowly and distinctly: "Why did you say *knew?*"

"She took off. You know how kids do."

"Why are you showing me this tape?"

He wouldn't quite look at me. "That's—part of what I want you to do."

Time for caution. I took refuge in another blank stare.

"You gotta find the original tape."

No I don't. I may have to stand under streetlights swinging my plastic purse, but I won't run errands for producers—especially not for Hummel. I said as much.

Hummel essayed a calm, grave look, as he does when he's about to Relate Meaningfully: "No kidding, Stoney. A very nice lady and a personal friend of mine has trouble."

Hummel's use of my nickname increased my suspicion. "I thought the girl disappeared."

"I mean *Denise* Tolman, her mother. Someone wants her to pay fifty thou for the original tape."

"The original's probably film. Looks like Ektachrome."

He waved away this picky technicality. "Point is, the tape shows her kid screwing somebody."

"That's not worth fifty thousand dollars. Not these days."

"Denise thinks so."

"Have her tell the police."

"She wants to keep it like quiet." He leveled sincere, ceramic eyes: "Stoney, you know the town, the Industry. You get things done. Denise wants *you*."

"She does not; she barely knows me. You sold her on me, Hummel. Why?"

A long pause, during which Hummel's struggle for plausibility was a minor pleasure to watch. Then he brightened: "She asked me who's the smartest guy around and I just had to say Stoney Winston."

"Flattery does not become you, Harry."

"She'll pay six bills a week for two weeks."

"I have a job here."

"Not anymore." I stood up quickly and Hummel added, "But you get it back in two weeks."

"You have six cola spots in production."

"Big deal. I'll direct them myself."

"No."

"Okay, big shot: you're fired anyway. I'm sick of your smart-ass face."

A reflective pause while my bankbook flashed before my eyes. "All right, I'll go talk to Denise Tolman."

"Whatever. Listen: do a good job and I'll still let you cut the spots."

"Let joy be unconfined."

"What?"

Chugging out to Pasadena in my ratty lemon Rabbit: through the tunnels, over the river—a foot-wide piddle in a concrete trough—and up the ancient freeway in the crisp September light.

I was conning myself into accepting the inescapable: thinking about two glorious expense-paid weeks away from Harry Hummel. No dreary trips to Malibu, no sand-filled shoes, no self-disgust at lavishing my attention on Cutrate Cola. A two-week reprieve before I had to start hustling again.

I eased around a '55 Porsche, now too valuable to be pushed to freeway speed.

I think I met Denise Tolman once: a Pasadena matron in preppie clothes. Her uncomplaining husband ran a little studio until cancer killed him. She needed the business to fund her Junior League life-style but wasn't interested in running it. So she hired a manager and resumed good works in Pasadena.

A '67 "Chebbie" whistled by, rear end barely two inches off the concrete, full of Mexican-American kids in identical T-shirts.

I don't know: porno tapes, extortion threats, disappearances—dangerous stuff, the lot.

But interesting. Maybe get some ideas for a script. Oh sure: to join all the others in my drawer.

San Rafael Circle turned out to be one street away from the Arroyo Seco—the gulch that holds the Rose Bowl. Expensive houses in the usual California mix: Revised Ranch, Retrained Colonial, Recycled Mansart. Not quite the Tudor forts and stone palazzi of the really rich a block away, but not loose change either. Denise Tolman's home squatted at the end of a long, narrow driveway, with a shake roof, green shutters, and ivy everywhere. I parked my seedy Rabbit beside a Mercedes coupe and rang the doorbell. The Rabbit's electric radiator fan was still whirring and I imagined it whispering to the Mercedes, "Pssst! The Fuehrer lives! Pass it on."

A touch of paranoia there. In forty years, the Reich has menaced nothing but Detroit. But I was born in England a few years after the war and childhood attitudes die hard. Sergeant-Major Winston ws my father's title then. He named me Spencer Churchill Winston in a peculiar fit of patriotic humor. But "Stoney Winston" now attracts no notice and I've schooled myself to speak in bland Los Angeles, as if I were an immigrant from Kansas.

Denise Tolman opened the door, dressed in jeans and denim shirt, a garden trowel in hand. Hazel eyes in an indistinctly pretty face. Hair a bit too uniformly blond and pants a shade too tight, as if she'd bought the size she hoped she still could fit. Ten years ago, she'd have been a delicious sorority girl with a peachy bloom and bouncing hair. Even now, after a decade of fighting gravity, she was ripely charming. But her soft face and chirpy voice were still back in that sorority, ten years gone.

Ten years? Fifteen at most. How could she have a grown daughter?

She led the way past ten thousand dollars' worth of colonial furniture and out into a vast back yard, where I dropped into a redwood chair beside the pool.

"I'm so glad you came out here, Stoney."

"Hummel said he'd fire me if I didn't."

Wry brackets around her mouth showed she knew Hummel's courtly ways. "Did Harry tell you what it's all about?"

"He played the tape."

Denise troweled a hole in a flower bed, inserted a bulb of indeterminate species, and filled the hole again. "I saw some of it. I couldn't watch very much."

"I understand."

"I hope you can find the original tape." I waited out another little burial. "Harry says you know everything about the Industry: every scene shop, soundstage, and prop house in town. He says that's why you're a good production manager."

"I'm a director."

Denise interred another bulb.

"Where is Lee now?"

Denise appeared to sift possible answers, then lifted her hands: "I wish I knew. I walked into her room one day with an armful of clothes to put away. She never put away her clothes—did you ever know a girl that did?" Denise flashed a cute smile, as if from habit. "And she was gone. Empty drawers and closets—well no, she never took her best dresses—but everything else, even little pictures off the walls. The note said sort of, well, 'good-bye' and 'thanks' and—that was it." Denise scooped another hole.

"How long ago was that?"

"About eight months." She sculpted the hole, rounding it to perfection, as if to plant a soup can. "And I don't know why."

"Do you want me to find your daughter?"

"She was Roy's daughter." Denise enlarged the hole to fit a coffee tin. "My husband divorced Lee's mother several years ago. She still lives up the coast, I think: Oxnard, Ventura—someplace like that. Pepe'd know."

"Pepe?"

"Pepe Delgado, my studio manager. He used to make out her alimony checks." A mournful smile. "Until Roy died."

That explained how a woman her age could have a grown daughter. "I wondered where her red hair came from. Well, do you want me to find Lee?"

She stared into the hole for a long moment, then sighed. "I guess she's eighteen, now. Maybe Lee wasn't happy here." She buried another bulb.

I changed the subject: "Denise, I know that tape distresses you, but why is it worth so much money?"

"Have you heard of Isiah Hammond?"

"He runs a fundamentalist church in Burbank. Does a lot of TV."

"A lot of movies too—mainly Bible stories. They show them on sheets in church basements."

"And he makes the movies on your lot."

"All the time. About half my income last year."

"So they threaten to show the tape to the righteous Reverend Hammond. Do you think he'd yank his production from your studio?"

"Those awful people: they scream if a TV actress doesn't wear a bra. I'm just afraid to take chances."

"Hm. How did the extortioner contact you?"

"Somebody called me, and a tape arrived in the mail."

"How are you to pay the money?"

"I don't know yet. They say they'll get back to me."

I stood up. "Why me? Why haven't you called the police?"

"I almost did, but I thought about it. Suppose they caught them. There'd be publicity and Hammond would hear about it anyway." She rose, stabbing her trowel into the new little plot. "I can't afford that, Stoney. That crummy studio is all Roy—all I've got. And Pepe says nobody else wants to shoot there."

I'd worked on her lot, and recalling that cramped little warren, I could believe her. "I've never tried to find anyone before."

"I don't want you to find people. I just want the tape. Please, Stoney, you're all I can think of."

Her body language said "Poor Helpless Me," but the stress in her face was real enough. She'd lost her husband and her stepdaughter, and now her livelihood was about to leak away.

Whatever I did, it couldn't be just a junket—a two-week respite from horrible Hummel. "I'll have to think about it. I can't take your money for nothing. If there's a chance I can find the tape, I'll give it a shot."

"You can find it."

"I'll call you tomorrow."

"No, come back and tell me. We'll talk about it."

She offered her hand and, when I shook it, deposited bits of flower bed in my palm.

"Oh!" Smiling, flustered, she took my wrist and scraped my hand across her denim sleeve. "Tomorrow."

Piloting the Rabbit through the interchange they call "The Stack" (in helicopter shots, its concrete branches swarm with metal aphids), I struggled up the Hollywood Freeway, reviewing the conversation with Denise.

I braked as an open semi groaning with produce whipped into line ahead of me. A vegetable dislodged, bounced off the concrete, smacked my grill. I'd killed a tomato.

Appealing woman, Denise—I mean *person*.

A sweet Grandma painted on a building side regarded me gravely as I passed. I assure you, Madam, this is simply business. Grandma looked unconvinced. Oh all right: appealing *woman*.

The issue was that tape. If I could find it, I'd actually earn the money. Maybe I could spot something in it that shows where it was made. Better have a look.

Through the open gate at Finart Studios (One-Arm Willard had left to resume his nap at home) and over to Hummel's rented bungalow. His crimson Eldorado was gone, so Harry was home too, or out breathing on girls. I opened his dreary office, started up the video rig, and concentrated:

INTERIOR BEDROOM NIGHT

1. FULL SHOT: Rear view. Athletic male kneel-

ing on bed, back to camera, between flapping knees of redheaded supine girl.

CUT TO:

2. WAIST SHOT: Her point of view. Her partner's a towheaded, straight-nosed surfing son with a face as blank as a cue ball.

CUT TO:

3. INSERT: The gynecological details.

CUT TO:

4. CLOSE-UP: The surfer's point of view. Lee Tolman's head and shoulders against the sheet.

CUT TO:

5. FULL SHOT: Rear view as before. The girl revolves onto knees and elbows, pelvis cocked like a puppy with tail in the air and front paws on a bone.

CUT TO:

6. TIGHT CLOSE-UP: Lee's face rhythmically pressing the sheet.

And so on and so forth at tedious length, this glorious old communion reduced to damp machinery. How anyone finds this erotic eludes me.

Distracted by these doggy rhythms, the mind wanders: how typical she is: pale, sloping breasts, slender arms and shanks, wall-to-wall freckles—except for the protected rump, where cool-white skin laps around the odd coral pimple, the single atoll mole.

These redheads: Irish, Danish, German, Pole; Gentile, Jew, and God knows what—a secret clan breeding true for centuries across countries and even races. Only three great families even now: Reddish Blond at one extreme; Irish Setter at the other; and in between, your Classic Carrot.

Like this girl: even her pubic hair's a hard, even orange—the too-perfect color of a nylon rug.

*   *   *

As I sat there sunk in pseudo-anthropology, the dreary images chased across the tube: FULL SHOT, CLOSE-UP, MEDIUM SHOT, CLOSE-UP . . . Only the close-ups seemed to register: Lee— Lee— Lee— Her face serenely strange under its carrot cloud; soft green gemstone eyes focused at infinity. Intercut with the other shots, her meditative face rebuked her wagging, spastic body.

I froze a close-up by chance as she glanced at the camera. The great green eyes watched me patiently; the face asked: why are you looking?

Because you've got me hooked.

Nonsense: she's just a girl in a sleazy film. The right freeze-frame makes *anyone* look eerie.

No, not "eerie"; something more. There was an odd transparency that gave the illusion of looking below the skin, beneath the skull, into a singular, sexless, inner beauty. She was beautiful, but she wasn't, but she *was*— and even frozen on the grainy little screen, she oscillated back and forth, compellingly. I stared for half a minute, as still as she was, then shook her image out of my head.

I jabbed the *pause* button and the ritual coupling resumed.

Hm: a truck shot; that meant a dolly. Four, maybe five lights—and up high too. No ceiling. Looked like a set. A studio.

Denise's studio? Well, it was a place to start. Maybe I *could* find Lee—I mean find the film.

In and out, in and out. Awful stuff. Ugh; enough. Profoundly depressed, I ejected the tape, returned the tawdry office to darkness, then pointed the Rabbit home to Laurel Canyon.

East Hollywood was snoozing in the late orange light: bungalows and stucco flats and unmarked warehouses hiding obscure goods. A frail grandma was pushing home a giant supermarket cart bearing two tiny parcels full of supper.

The Angelus.

*   *   *

I was still evading Lee's green-eyed gaze when I got home to find my young landlady on her knees in the flowers beside the drive. Plants: in pots, plots, boxes, beds, and barrels, L.A. plants obsessively.

"Hi, Sally."

She sat up and grinned, displaying a T-shirt emblazoned "GOOD AND PLENTY!" The candy box depicted was contorted into a topologist's erotic dream.

"Aren't you uncomfortable without your undies?"

She pushed at her damp, Viking hair. "Nope, I took the *Cosmopolitan* test."

"The what?"

"They ran an article on how to tell if you could go braless." She stood up, dusting her hands on filthy shorts. "See, you take a pencil and push it up under your breast."

"Ow!"

"*Horizontally*, dimbulb. If you can't hold the pencil, you stick out enough to do without a bra. If the pencil stays there, you're too droopy."

"And what was your result?"

"Do you realize how *male* this whole discussion is? Listen: I made lasagna."

"Do you realize how female that transition was?"

Sally ignored this feeble face-saving. "What do you say? I've got a ton of it."

"I don't know, Sally. . . ."

"Well, see how you feel later. I'm going to go shower. I'm all stuck together." She tugged at her damp T-shirt and the candy box approached its normal shape.

Sally was built to special order for Wagner or Renoir, whose taste I most certainly share; and our dinners often lead to other things that are fun too.

Oh hell. To be honest, I love Sally, obsessively, foolishly—and without encouragement. She chortles at my smart remarks and pats my arm in passing as we cook rich suppers in her warm kitchen. She shows me the sardonic wit she can't reveal at work. And when we wander off to bed, she wraps me in an embrace so comprehensive it engulfs me, soul and body.

But in the morning she rises cheerfully to resume a life as disconnected from mine as if we'd simply shared a bus seat.

Drives me nuts.

Sally ambled toward the house, still cleaning her hands on her khaki behind. She'd got the hillside cottage in a divorce settlement and rented me the downstairs flat to help pay the mortgage. Considering my income, her choice was ill-advised.

I descended eight steps to my front door, dreading the evening routine. Today's mail: three final notice bills and an offer to sell me desert property:

"YES! **Mr. S. Wimpston,** You are a WINNER!!!"

I unlocked the flimsy door and trudged into my dank, empty cave: cinderblock bookcases on the left wall, floor to ceiling and corner to corner. Back wall mostly hidden by my photographs in snap-together frames. Living room paved with dirty clothes. I waded through them to the TV set to check the guide: zilch. Over to the kitchen on the right-hand side to consult the fridge: ditto. Dispensing the last can of beer. Adding today's wardrobe to the bedroom floor and into the bathroom, which was redolent of mildew. Its only virtue is a walk-in shower.

The apartment shows the misplaced enterprise of Sally's former husband. He'd fixed it up to rent for several hundred a month. But since it's half buried in the hillside, the back rooms are almost windowless and the seeping winter rains paint Rorschachs on the walls. I got it cheap.

I wet the rigid washcloth: hm, a trifle ripe, as usual. Better soap it extra hard. Clanking pipes—another drawback—revealed Sally in her own shower overhead, lathering her abundance as promised. I turned on my own shower.

"SONOFABITCH!" came through the ceiling.

Oops. The sudden water pressure drop guaranteed that Sally's abundance was now slightly scalded. Under my own water, meditating on the scene above: Sally scrubbing, snorting in the spray. Slippery trickles snaking down her back. Cornsilk hair plastered to her brown neck. Singing "When I'm Sixty-Four" in a brazen, female baritone.

Maybe I should reassess that dinner invitation.

Sure, to eat her food and share her day and listen to some Mozart in the dusk; to bloody my head against her wall of independence.

Standing in the musty stall, I watched the runoff eddy around my big feet.

Still, after a day of Harry Hummel, Denise Tolman, and passive, puzzled Lee, I needed to be around a grown-up.

And Sally was eminently qualified.

2

SANTA ANA LIGHT THE NEXT MORNING ON THE WAY BACK to Pasadena, as desert winds drove out the smog and sucked the air dry. Hillside houses snapped into phony 3-D Technicolor and the sky was a perfect cyclorama. The view was breathtaking but subtly unconvincing—an elaborate model shot. Eighty degrees at nine AM and the hard glare promised twenty more by noon.

I pursued a favorite pastime as I drove: conversing with imaginary passengers. Today my spectral guest was Woody Allen.

He regarded the surreal landscape balefully through his horn-rims: "L.A. Wonderful; my favorite place. Who built those houses, Mattel?"

"You get used to them."

"Sartre was wrong, believe me. Hell is Southern California."

"For some people."

"Look what it did to you. You used to be English, like Matthew Arnold or Virginia Woolf. But now, who could tell?"

"It's just my tan."

"If a tan is so important, take a cruise." Woody leveled large, sad eyes: "You know you're doomed? First your legs atrophy, then you start telling everyone to 'have a good one.' Before you know it, you're breathing through your mouth. Jesus, watch it!" He clutched his armrest spastically as the Rabbit hurtled around a Buick piloted by a serene grandma too short to see over her steering wheel. The armrest came off in his hand.

15

"At least there's freedom here."

"Freedom for what: to dry your brain like a raisin? Where're we going?"

"Pasadena."

He groaned, his worst suspicions confirmed: "California hell. And with my luck, I'll spend eternity watching the Rose Parade. Listen, just *being* here is unbelievably stressful. Why are you putting me through this?"

"I need advice. If you had to investigate something, how would you do it?"

"Like Nero Wolfe: I'd stay in New York—*indoors*. Look, that's not really the problem, so what do you say we get right to it."

"It's the girl in the film."

"Better; much better. What about her?"

"She's reaching me."

"How?"

"She looks so ethereal. How could she make a film like that?"

Woody nodded until his specs bounced on his nose. "Okay. Right. Suddenly it's clear: you have this fantastic landlady—"

"How did Sally get in this?"

"A fantastic person—I mean we are talking borderline implausible: smart, together, with a body some teenage boy dreamed up in the dark."

"Look—"

"She feeds you, talks to you, sleeps with you; she even *likes* you. But you want more and she won't give it. So you get back at her: you develop an obsession with this movie chick who is spiritual on top but carnal on the bottom and adjacent parts. This obsession is irrational; maybe neurotic. So to rationalize it, you ask me, the Fellini of flaky females."

"The Allen of alliteration."

"Don't evade the issue, which is, you have a problem: you're determined to be hooked on a girl you never met; you can't reconcile what she looks like with what she's doing in that film; and you can't admit the combination pressurizes your pants."

"Hey!"

"Come *on:* the whorehouse madonna, the slime angel—I have to tell you these oxymorons are old hat. On top of which, you're leching at her mother too."

"Stepmother."

"So technically it's not incest. Technically." He shook his head with weary sympathy. "My friend, you live a highly developed fantasy life, and so what, who doesn't? But you're in very great danger of confusing it with reality. Listen: I gotta split; this air is killing my sinuses."

"Thanks for the advice—I guess."

His spindly form was becoming transparent. "I'll give you one more piece: be totally careful, Winston. *This is not a game.*"

Woody vanished.

Denise Tolman stood at the maple table in her bright yellow breakfast room, snipping food coupons out of the newspaper. A button-down shirt in a tablecloth check this morning, plus tight jeans whose pocket stitching presumably sent status messages to those who could decode them. I couldn't.

She didn't look at me as I spoke: "Denise, I've decided to take the job."

Her contour-handled scissors snickered out a coffee coupon, which she added to a growing pile.

I tried again: "Since Lee is in that tape, she has to know who shot it. So the obvious plan is to find her."

The scissors hesitated, then stalked an orange juice discount.

"You have no idea where she went?"

Denise scanned the paper for more prey.

"The tape was probably shot in a studio."

The scissors darted after new quarry.

"Maybe your studio. It's a place to start looking."

Her face tightened. "Don't go there."

"I'll just say you asked me to find her. I don't have to mention the tape."

"Please don't go." She sifted coupons, counting the day's haul.

"Look Denise: you're paying me for two weeks. Now I can relax at the beach and phone in fairy tales or I can get that tape back. Which is it to be?"

"Maybe I'll try the market up on Linda Vista."

"Denise!"

She looked at me as if she'd walked into a store and then forgotten what she'd come for.

"Denise, what is the matter?"

She picked up a shoulder bag covered with pockets; unzipped a pocket; zipped the pocket; unzipped another; folded her cuttings; stored them deliberately; zipped the pocket. "I thought I had a Cheerios coupon."

Perhaps this arid light had driven her round the bend. They say Santa Ana winds unglue people. Circling the table, I grasped her arms gently, just below her shoulders.

"Anybody home?"

A six-second freeze-frame, then her left eye extruded one fat teardrop, which struggled through an eyelash, plopped into the faint depression at the bottom of her eye socket, then made a stately progress down her plump cheek. It seemed to take an hour. Even in the air conditioning, she exuded a certain warm femaleness, mixed with breakfast smells.

"What's wrong, Denise?"

She scraped at the tear track with an index finger, then made an interminable job of refolding the newspaper. Finally: "I'm sorry I got upset."

"Why don't you want me to go to your studio?"

"The church group's shooting there today."

"I won't talk to them. But it's logical to start at the studio. Did Lee ever go there?"

"Yes—well, not often. I don't know."

"Hm. Tell me about the extortion."

"Someone called and said I'd be getting a tape in the mail. For my own good, I'd better play it. I don't have a recorder, so when the tape came, I took it to Harry."

"Why Hummel?"

"Harry and I are friends." The dropped eyelashes suggested more than friendship. "I was shocked by the tape, of course. I mean, I never even saw a hard-core movie. And when I recognized Lee . . ."

"What happened next?"

"She called back and said she wanted fifty thousand dollars or Isiah Hammond would see the tape."

"She?"

"It was a woman. Remember how I said Hammond gives me half my business? Well it's more than just half—it's really most of it. That's why I'm so worried."

"But you didn't want to pay."

"Fifty thousand dollars?" Her eyes and voice filled up again. "That's four months' gross. And with the overhead, there's nothing left. Thank God Roy had mortgage life insurance on this house or I'd be out on the street with my furniture."

"Did the caller sound like Lee, by any chance?"

Denise looked surprised. "Maybe."

"Did you recognize her voice?"

"No. Why do you think it was Lee?"

My turn to play with the newspaper, while phrasing a diplomatic reply. "Yesterday, you hinted that you and your stepdaughter didn't get along. Could Lee be getting back at you for something?"

She clenched her lips to stop their trembling. Then: "I hope not. I really tried so hard with her."

I didn't push it. "Okay, Denise, call your studio manager and say I'm coming. I think we can sort this out."

Moving close to me, Denise stared hard at my face, switching her gaze back and forth as if to verify that my two eyes matched. "I hope so, Stoney. I don't have to tell you what this means to me."

*   *   *

I swung the Rabbit off the freeway at Santa Monica Boulevard and rattled past the sex shops and porno movies around Western Avenue, toward Denise's tiny studio, a block off Santa Monica. The dusty brown soundstage wall proclaimed "Tolman Studios" in faded paint. "Studios" was stretching it for a tired stucco hangar equipped with a dwarf lobby, a rental bay full of lights and grip equipment, and a few mangy cubicles for editing and offices. The soundstage itself was barely big enough for shooting commercials and the entire lot wasn't a fifth the size of Finart Studios six blocks west, where Hummel rents his office.

I zipped into the front parking lot, which was unguarded by a gate, and penned the Rabbit in a space lettered "21st Century Enterprises"—a commercial production house that expired four years back.

A relief to exchange the surreal sunshine outside for the silent gloom within. I padded down a dingy corridor lit by egg crate fluorescents, heaved open the massive, padded door, and stepped into the tiny soundstage.

The usual tableau: foreground confusion of lights, chairs, and lounging technicians silhouetted by the lit set behind them: a tent contrived from draperies and dressed with potted palms. An imposing gent in Sunday School pageant costume being patted by a squatty makeup man. An Isiah Hammond show, no doubt.

The fat, weary director was fighting with the camera man: "Whaddya got?"

"Too high. I can see the floor."

"Oh hell, you gotta boom down for this shot."

"What can I say? The floor is in the frame."

"Well tilt up; I mean, Jesus."

"I'll lose him."

"Hell. Satch!" The key grip uncoiled from a chair and ambled up.

"Get him a half-apple."

The key grip produced a blue wooden box. Old Testament Grandpa climbed aboard.

"How's that?"

"Now he's out of his key."

"Hell. Enders!" Now the gaffer headed toward the key light with all deliberate speed. He began adjusting it as I retreated to the hall and climbed the musty stairs to the second floor offices.

Pepe Delgado was a very busy manager. He signed three letters (first shaking back a gold wrist chain), banged a ledger shut, and dropped a stack of papers in his OUT basket, displacing a puff of dust.

"Pepe . . ."

"One moment." He keyed the antique intercom: "Hold my calls!"

"Nobody's out there."

"No? Ah. Perhaps the girl went to lunch." He shot his cuffs, clasped his hands, and smiled. "Now: my undivided attention."

"Denise Tolman asked me to find her daughter."

"She is a nice lady, that one."

"How about her daughter Lee?"

Pepe mimed "remembering," eyes beseeching Heaven, pursed lips lifting his little mustache horizontal, painful cogitation.

Finally: "I don't recall her."

"You've never met her?"

Pepe was about as Mexican as a plastic taco, but he saw himself as Ricardo Montalban. He hunched thin, velour-coated shoulders in a Latin shrug: "That is what I said, my friend."

"And you're certain she never came to this studio?"

"I am sorry, my friend; I am too busy to keep track of visitors."

I was already tired of being Pepe's friend. "Denise said you had the address of Roy Tolman's first wife."

"I guess I got it someplace, but it is three years old."

"I'll take it anyway."

"It might be in my files."

"Would you get it for me please?"

"My pleasure." He pronounced it to rhyme with *pressure*.

He didn't move. Neither did I. We waited.

Finally, with another shrug and a windy sigh, Pepe went to a filing cabinet and, striking a reflective pose, depicted "remembering" again. Then, with a eureka! flourish, he pulled the top drawer, rose on dainty tiptoes to augment his five feet-four, and scanned the folders. He yanked one out.

"Rachel Gershon: 1229 Sea Vista, Ventura."

"Phone?"

Pepe smiled with sour pleasure: "No listing." Tossing the folder at the file drawer, he swept across to his office door and opened it with ostentatious meaning.

"I may want to ask some questions later, Pepe."

"I will attempt to fit you in." He shut the door behind me.

"The girl's" desk was still vacant when I crossed the outer office, except for a two-year-old calendar. One of those long lunches.

Back down the creaking stairs and into the soundstage, just in time for a take. The assistant camera man extended the slate one-handed, two fingers holding the clapstick open.

"Speed."

"Mark it."

The sound man muttered into the mike beside his Nagra recorder, "Sixteen baker take three." *Clack!* The assistant scuttled back to the Eclair camera, ready to pull focus.

"And action."

Grandpa struck a hortatory pose, intoning, "*And when Jehu was come to Jezreel, Jezebel heard of it; and she painted her face, and tired her head, and looked out at a window.*"

The delivery was somewhere between old Finlay Currie and John Huston at his most oracular: "*And he said, 'Throw her down.' So they threw her down: and some of her*" *blood was sprinkled on the wall, and on the horses: and he trode her underfoot."*

"Trode?"

The key grip twisted a dolly knob and the camera crept silently downward. *"'Go, see now this cursed woman, and bury her: for she is a king's daughter.'"*

The key grip eased the crab dolly back from the actor while the assistant pulled focus. *"And they went to bury her: but they found no more of her than the skull, and the feet, and the palms of her hands."*

The script girl followed the text with a pencil, mouthing each word. *"And the carcase of Jezebel shall be as dung upon the face of the field in the portion of . . .* what? What's that word?"

"Holy Jesus, cut!"

Grandpa's voice lost thirty years and twenty DB of bass: "The goddam dolly blocked my cue card."

"Take four right away."

But the assistant carolled, "Reload!"

"Oh Christ!"

I gathered the Rev. Hammond was not on the set today.

I latched the massive soundstage door and turned back into the corridor to confront a girl clacking toward me in high-heeled boots. She made a stirring long shot but did not quite survive the close-up: chestnut pageboy wig, lashes like tufts of blacking brush, deltas of umber makeup faking cheekbones. Sleeveless undershirt under a Kit Carson fringed jacket and jeans so tight they squeezed her flesh into small parentheses bracketing her hips. She carried a Lucite tray like a cigarette girl in a gangster picture.

She looked at the door. "They making one?"

"Red light's off. They're reloading." The little tray compartments were packed with pills, tablets, lozenges, capsules—tan, brown, white, and olive—in every size from pinheads to stream pebbles.

She saw me looking. "Vitamins."

"All of them?"

"Yeh really; and minerals and protein concentrate—stuff like that. Oh hell." She pursed sticky lips at the now-revolving light beside the door. "They're shooting again." She clopped into a room opposite the soundstage door and dropped the tray on a table.

I followed. "What are they for?"

Under the android makeup, her smile was sweetly natural. "I'm a consultant like. See, I find out about your health and eating habits and stuff and then I prescribe vitamins."

"Quite a variety."

"Well sure. Natural health is real hard, cause we're so corrupt." I blinked. "I mean our eating and health and stuff. How's your sex life? Oh it's okay; I'm like a doctor, right? Nothing personal."

"Why do you ask?"

She picked out a translucent pill full of yellow goop. "Know what this is?"

"Vitamin E?"

"Mainly, but this is different; exclusive. See those grains? Pot. Female essence. Dynamite stuff."

"A personal testimonial?"

She frowned, struggling with the idea, then grinned. Like her smile, her teeth were engagingly natural and slightly crooked. "You got a great vocabulary. I respect that. Hey, is Pepe on the floor?"

"He was upstairs in his office. Is Pepe a client?"

"Yeh, I'm working on his wind—like he cuts it a lot, you know? Embarrassing. I'm trying vitamin C."

I considered this therapy gravely, then: "Do you have a business card?"

"Naw. I'm Peeper Martin."

"Stoney Winston."

"A cowboy name—only you don't look like one." She shook my hand with cheerful vigor.

"Peeper, I'm doing some work for Denise Tolman. She owns this lot. I'm looking for her daughter, Lee."

"Official?" The candor washed out of her face. "Hey listen: she's got a right to live her life."

"You bet she does. I just need to find her to give her money." Peeper relaxed slightly. "Denise, uh, had an offer to sell the studio and of course Lee would be involved."

I was pleased with this improvisation, but it only revived Peeper's wariness. "She gonna sell the lot?"

"Just an offer. Maybe nothing to it."

"Yeh, well I gotta see Pepe—I mean about his vitamins." She stepped out into the hall.

"Where can I find Lee?"

Peeper stood quite still, looking at me from under her sticky eyelashes. Then she walked slowly back into the room. "You know, you send funny waves." Like Denise earlier, she stared into my eyes, one at a time. "Kinda smartass—but positive."

I looked at her, intrigued by this nice chipper person disguised as a tart, like a happy child in a Halloween suit. As if still reading those waves of mine, she snapped her gawky grin.

"Try the fag."

"Not an exclusive label in these parts."

"Um, Wishbourne. Candy Wishbourne. Are you ready for that name?"

"I know Candy; the art director."

"Right; well, she talked about him sometimes." Peeper grabbed her tray of nostrums.

"Thanks. Say, do those things earn you a living?"

She cocked the tray on her hip and posed. "Naw, I'm a movie star." Then she clattered off up the hall, obviously hot to tell Pepe that Denise was selling the lot.

Lying on the water bed in Sally's twilit bedroom, playing stethoscope: my right ear pillowed on her warm sternum, cycling slowly up and down like an anchored boat. I was listening to her romantic heartbeat and the more prosaic burbles of her supper, processing.

My right eye was blinded by flesh, leaving my left one to interpret Sally's contours without benefit of depth perception. From my worm's-eye angle, I traced a vast Saharan landscape of dunes undulating toward a tiny, golden cloud so distant it might have been a mirage, hovering at the base of foothill thighs.

Rocked by Sally's gentle breath and lulled by muffled peristalsis, I was slipping into a light doze.

"Am I putting you to sleep?"

"Wha? Oh! No, I'm tracking every word. You said he was worried about peripherals."

Sally was rehearsing the incomprehensible details of her day at work, selling computers. "You *did* hear me. But when I told him what you could do with an RS232 port, I really turned him around. I *know* I'm going to land that order." Sally's one of the best salesmen in her region.

She scratched my back and the tan landscape danced a gentle hula. "That'll put my year-to-date way over last year's. Hey! Then we could take a vacation." Excited, she wrapped her arm about me so I was pillowed fore and aft.

"Stoney, are you listening?"

"Had my earmuffs on." Sally smelled of sunshine and apples.

"About a vacation?"

"Let's get married instead."

"No."

"Why not, Sally?"

"Same reason as last night."

The sting of it turned me defensive: "No vacation until I can pay half."

My resilient cave tensed around me. "Shove off!"

She swung out of bed and thudded into the kitchen, a thoroughbred Clydesdale mare. The fridge door slammed and bottles clanked as she worked off her annoyance through excess percussion.

Laurel Canyon insects droned mantras in the dusk.

To be honest, there's no good reason why she should commit to me. When I work, I'm away on location half the time. And when I don't, I'm down at Unemployment.

Which is partly why she earns three times what I do.

She can rent my head and body for a kind word and a plate of pasta, so why should she pay upkeep and depreciation on me?

Winston is not cost-effective.

Sally returned with fresh bottles of Dos Equis beer and stretched out at right angles across the head of the bed.

Dank silence while we sucked our beers.

"I'm sorry, Sally, but you can't have it both ways. You can't be independent if I'm *de*pendent."

"Your ego can't stand living off a mere woman."

I rose on one elbow to scan the length of her. "I'd call you anything but 'mere.'"

"You mean fat."

Oversensitive. In fact, Sally has just enough substance to look properly female: a subtle, ripe convexity. I lay back, pillowed on her middle.

"Though I do wish the bloody Industry would let me earn a living."

My head bounced with Sally's chuckle. "Bloody. You don't often use British words."

"I'm not British—haven't been for half my life."

"But you're not quite American either." She sat upright. "What *are* you?"

A long pause while the crickets went on vamping in the trees beyond the deck outside. What was I? Small-bore thinker, would-be artist, poser, floater, detached from my own culture and shipped off to be the purest kind of Californian; an immigrant to a nation-state.

"Let's say I'm prone to self-dramatizing."

Sally ignored that. "Why did you leave England?"

"Not my choice; I was just a kid. When my mother got fed up with being an army wife, she took me as far away as possible. I guess Los Angeles was the best she could think of, this side of Kuala Lumpur."

And my old dad got emergency leave to fly to L.A. where he pleaded with her to come back and then wept alone in my dark bedroom before flying back and disappearing from my life.

As if she sensed my feelings, Sally wrapped her arms around her knees, trapping my head completely.

"You're flattening my ears."

She released me and I rolled over to lie on my back beside her.

"Sorry I overreacted to your vacation offer."

"Okay." She got up on her knees, planted a palm on either side of me, and started a slow reverse push-up. "Cootchy-coo, Stoney." She swung back and forth, back and forth, upside-down bells tolling gently.

"And I promise to lighten up."

"Shut up, Stoney."

Sally descended like summer twilight.

3

Tracing screechy turns through the Hollywood Hills on this bright morning, which was indistinguishable from yesterday's because L.A. dispenses weather in job lots, often weeks at a time. I needed to check out Candy Wishbourne, who lived up here in the hills near the end of this semi-rural road, in a neighborhood so rife with sodomites they call it "Lavender Hill."

I struggled past Candy's driveway, missing the ceramic tile house number blushing pink below matching hibiscus. Half a mile to a turnaround, then slowly back. Down a patched concrete driveway to a sixty-year-old house built in Conquistador Cute: red tile roof, tan stucco troweled in rustic sweeps, picture window shaped liked a MacDonald's arch, oak door with outsized iron hinges and a spy hole, which opened to my knock on a yellow eye.

"Candy in?"

A beat, then the eye tracked indolently down the six feet-two of me from straggling hair to sneakers, inspecting my thinnish, beaky nose, assertive chin, and frame which Sally insists is not, in fact, skinny. The eye paused appreciatively at my scrimshaw belt buckle but dismissed my nobrand jeans with a flicker.

The spy hole closed; the door opened. "Yes?"

"I'm Stoney Winston, a director. Candy knows me."

Cerberus was five feet-four, with a black, quarter-inch crew cut and a gold stud in one earlobe. A sparrow body in red tank top and faded cutoffs. Feet bare. His thin face had stopped evolving during adolescence, but his eyes belonged to a hotel doorman or an aging cop.

"I'll get him." His voice was incongruous: an actor's basso. He left me in the tiny foyer, surveying the gilt mirror and the floor of black and white parquet so overscale that two and a half squares spanned the hall.

"Hel-*lo* sailor!" Candy gives the Straights a show of Gay clichés until they pass some private test of his.

"Hey, Candy. Saw your beer commercial last week. Nice job."

"The driveler who lit my set made it look two feet deep." But Candy seemed pleased that I'd noticed. Recognizing me, he dropped the Oscar Wilde impression. "Come in, dear boy; always a treat to chat with an adult."

I followed him through an archway to the Spanish colonial living room. Once he accepts you, Candy is a pleasure to work with: easy-going, considerate, and completely professional—with a bottomless fund of movie lore and a wit as dry as silica gel. In his habitual twill jumpsuit, he looks like a fat repairman, come to fix the fridge. As if to complete this image, he rolled a vacuum cleaner away from the white sofa, to let me sit down.

"Housekeeping's a cross I bear. Herbie abhors a vacuum—naturally." Turning to the Sparrow: "Don't you?"

Herbie stared, impassive.

"And what brings you up to Wuthering Heights?"

"Candy, do you know Denise Tolman?"

"No, but I've been on her lot many times."

"How about her stepdaughter, Lee?"

"Redheaded child? Mm-hm. Like some tea?"

"No thanks."

"Well I will, since hooch is now forbidden. Herbie, be a sweetheart." The Sparrow glared at the tone of command, but padded obediently into the kitchen. "I'm due for a spot of surgery and my picky doctor just insists on marginal liver function."

Come to think of it, Candy looked more grey and flaccid than ever, and his flaky hair was almost gone.

"What's this about Lee Tolman?"

"Denise is worried about her."

"Ah, the wicked stepmother."

"Why do you say that?"

"It's expected; though I must say Denise doesn't do a very good Witch of the West."

"I thought you didn't know her."

Candy waggled Groucho eyebrows: "I have my sources."

The Sparrow returned with tea in a flowery cup, the kind you assemble in sets, no two alike. Candy sipped, then puckered: "What is this bilge? I know: you put in saccharin. Ugh. He's trying to give me cancer."

"Redundant," Herbie muttered, retiring to the white piano stool.

"Candy, Denise is making some financial arrangements involving Lee." His skeptical eyebrows urged me forward. "Lee may have some money coming."

"She could use it. She hasn't a dime, as far as I know."

"Then you've seen her recently?"

"Here and there."

Unaccountably, I felt a billowing relief. "Is she all right?"

"Shouldn't she be? Dear boy, what is all this?"

"Lee moved out of Denise's home eight months ago and hasn't contacted her since. I've only seen—well, some pictures of her, but she seems very unworldly—vulnerable. She worries me."

Candy placed his cup and saucer on the marble coffee table between us and stirred his tea in small, majestic circles. I sat tight.

Finally, he looked up: "She stayed here for a while, with us."

"Here?"

"She was safe enough." His flat tone signalled my gaffe.

"I only meant, I didn't realize you knew her that well."

"Oh yes, she practically lived at the studio for a while. It was after her father died. She confided in me."

Herbie rumbled resentfully, "Her Dutch Aunt."

Candy ignored him. "Then she went to work for that Bible-thumper in Burbank, for about six months—until the good Christians fired her."

"Isiah Hammond's church?"

"The Universal Christian Church of Burbank, California. Nice cadence to it."

"Why'd they let her go?"

"Wouldn't tithe or something; who knows? Well, she'd no place to go and no money and she wouldn't go back to Pasadena—I mean, who would? So she came to Herbie and me."

"Is she still here?"

"Oh no. She left about two weeks ago, for fields and pastures new."

"She didn't say where?"

Candy shook his head, eyeing me as if trying to decide something. Then: "Lee's an extraordinary personality. Very quiet. Almost . . ."

". . . Mousey." Another footnote from Herbie.

"But she has a mesmerizing quality. Very hard to describe. I despise the term, but 'vibrations' comes to mind."

"I feel them myself."

"Then I would be doubly careful." With this cryptic remark, he set down his cup and leaned back.

Plainly, Candy was through volunteering, so I decided to take a small risk: "Did Lee have anything to do with porno films?"

He didn't blink: "Not the kind I watch." Zero for trying.

"I'm going to find her, Candy. Any suggestions?" He shook his head and rose. "Then do me one favor: give her my number if she comes back."

He took my business card. "If she . . . gets in touch, I'll tell her about your interest."

His line reading was peculiar, but I couldn't tell why. "Fair enough." I retreated to the black and white foyer, shadowed by Herbie. "Thanks, Candy. Hope your surgery goes well."

He semaphored a fat arm. "Not to worry: I know my liver redeemeth!"

Standing on the sullen Malibu beach, amazed as always that Los Angeles offers three weathers at once: crisp autumn on Candy Wishbourne's mountain, smoggy summer in the flats below, and now grey winter at the water's edge.

Hummel's crew ignored the dismal gloom. They were used to filming on location at great expense, then canceling the rented natural environment by erecting a studio around it. Just now, they were overpowering a small section of dismal afternoon with a golden summer sunset.

The gaffer (the crew's token female) moved from point to point, aiming the Spectra light meter's bulging eye back at the camera: "The fire itself is f-eleven; f-four overall—no, make it a hot four."

Cameraman: "Okay, pull the 85 filter. Wilma, lose the dikes and see if you can split five-six and eight around the fire." She pulled blue/gold glass filters from the banks of lights.

The talent lounged around the fire: Boy and Girl Next Door; Sexpot whose prosthetic cleavage should be named "Silicon Valley"; pudgy comic relief; and the obligatory Black Couple, a toffee fraternity president and a bikini-ed Zulu princess with a belly flat and shiny as a Steinway lid.

Hummel was pacing the strand with an expostulating client in water-stained loafers, trailed by a dim assistant with a clipboard. Too far away to hear them—even Hummel.

I'd returned from Candy Wishbourne's to find Hummel's civil request on my phone machine: "Get your ass out to Malibu. We're shooting the cola spots." Since I was on detached service to Denise Tolman, I thought I'd better go sort Hummel out. So here I was, shivering in the late afternoon fog, waiting to be summoned into the Presence.

Client and Clipboard wandered off, still gesticulating, and Hummel waved me forward like a traffic cop. I trudged past the prop man guarding ten cases of Product, skirted the laboring generator, and tramped down to Hummel at the water's edge.

"Where the hell ya been?"

"I love our little reunions, Harry."

"Jeez, I left a message hours ago. You knew we were shooting."

"*You're* shooting. I'm chasing feelthy pictures."

"Yeah, I wanna talk about that." He started along the surf line, expecting me to follow. Twenty yards on, he stopped. "You gotta . . . Where the hell are ya?" I took my time approaching. "Can't you keep up? Listen, I need you here on the shoot."

"But you're not paying me; Denise is."

"Yeah, well we worked that out. She'll let me have you like part-time."

"Only part-time; well, well. And she wasn't keen on having me visit her studio. What's happening, Harry?"

"Never mind. But she's right: you be careful about that."

"Why?"

His blank glare suggested mental struggle, then: "'Cause I said so." He stared at his shoes as if suddenly wondering why they were sandy. "Another thing: don't tell people you're looking for the kid."

"Why not?"

"Well, you're looking for the tape."

"And how do I explain that?"

"I dunno; who cares? Look: direct the shoot here, okay? Then you can start looking again."

"I'll check with Denise."

Hummel exploded: "The hell you will! You get your ass over there and set up the next goddam shot!"

"What shot?"

"I'll tell you when I'm ready."

"Then I'll wait."

"*Winston!!*" But the ocean claimed Hummel's attention by suddenly covering his shoes. "Oh holy shit Jesus!" He pranced away up the beach.

Slow deep breath time. "Hummel?"

He hopped back toward me. "Why the hell don't you look where you're going? How goddam dumb can you get?" He wiped at his shoes with pages from his shooting script.

"Hummel!"

"I mean, jeez, Winston; what do I have to . . ."

"Hummel. Shut. Up."

He froze, goggling.

"I'm quitting, Hummel."

"Huh?"

"I'm tired playing games."

"What?"

"First you needed me to direct your commercials; then you didn't; now you do again. Denise is so desperate to get that tape, she's half hysterical. But not desperate enough to keep me looking for it. You and she are 'friends,' a term fraught with ambiguity. . . ."

"What?"

". . . and the whole situation feels phony. So I'm quitting."

"You're getting paid."

"Sue me. Entail my worldly goods."

"What about the spots?"

"Yes, what about them? Two days ago, you didn't need me for them. Why am I suddenly so important?"

By now, Hummel's reactions were stacked up in a holding pattern too congested to let any land.

"And in this mood of constructive frankness, I should add that I won't be bullied by two-a-penny yahoos like you."

"Huh?"

"Let me rephrase that in your vernacular: *Harry, go shit in your hat!*"

Long, long pause—fade up wave and gull sound effects—while Hummel's face went through several skin-tightening exercises. Then: "Okay, okay. About the spots, well, I run into some trouble—hey, nothing I can't handle, right?—but, well, maybe you better direct."

"What about Denise?"

"I don't know, I swear. You gotta ask her that."

"No I don't."

"Call her, willya? Please!"

Please? From Hummel? It was my turn to goggle.

"She can tell you."

Ripple-dissolve to flashback of Denise, hand on my forearm, lone tear leaking down her cheek. Corny but potent.

"All right, Harry; but I'm still off the shoot."

"Whatever." Hummel took a deep breath, like an actor resuming his character before a take. "Okay, what're ya hanging around for? Get outa here!" He dismissed me with a sweeping turn and marched away toward the cast and crew around the fire.

Stuffed into a phone booth on Pacific Coast Highway, phone on one ear, finger in the other, to mute the traffic demonstrating Doppler effects ten feet away.

"Yes?"

"Hi, Denise; Stoney."

"What? Stoney! You sound like you're in a factory."

"Pay phone. Denise, Harry says you've called it off. Is that right?"

A considerable silence, then an almost pleading tone: "Stoney, *why* did you say I was selling the studio?"

"To give me a reason for being there. It seemed plausible."

"No wonder! Because I *am* selling it—well, trying to."

"Then what's wrong?"

"Harry told me not to talk about it. I don't have a firm buyer yet, and 'til I do, I have to keep production going. Harry says I'll never sell the lot if it's standing empty."

"I don't follow you, Denise."

"Oh Stoney, you're supposed to be smart. If my staff finds out, they'll leave for other jobs. I had a *terrible* time with Pepe after you told him."

"I didn't tell *him* exactly, but I see what you mean. All right, I'm sorry; it was an innocent mistake."

"I'm not criticizing, Stoney. I know how helpful you're being."

"Then why don't you want me looking for Lee?"

Another lengthy pause, then Denise said something in a voice too small to penetrate the passing traffic.

"Say again?"

"I can't tell you, Stoney. I'm afraid to."

"Afraid of what?"

"Please, Stoney. I'm sorry."

Click.

I stabbed the phone buttons savagely; brusque dialogue with the operator; receiver picked up again. Then silence.

"Denise? Is someone with you? If you can't talk now, say something phony—anything.

"Denise?"

Silence.

"Denise, I have to know you're all right, or I'll call the Pasadena police from here."

A mournful little sigh. "You're sweet, Stoney."

"What's wrong?"

"Oh, everything—but nothing special. Nobody's here. I'm safe as can be. Really."

Another gap while I fumbled for a way to get more out of her.

"But it's nice to know someone worries about me. It's been a while. Good-bye, Stoney."

Click.

Hummmmmm.

4

CREEPING ALONG PARALLEL TO THE VENTURA CITY BEACH, I peered at street signs through the foggy twilight. Right turn onto Sea Vista toward the ocean, past a jumble of bungalows, mini-ranches, and seaside caprices in every state from newly-built to near-collapse. Amiable curs shambled out of the Rabbit's path down the narrow lane to 1229, last on the right, where the street dead-ends on the sand. A distant jogger and her two romping mongrels owned the whole beach. Even the gulls had packed it in for the day.

Lee Tolman's mother lived in a pseudo-Tudor cottage with machine-cut half-timbering pasted on stucco, surrounded by a post-and-panel fence six feet high. Two dings on the little ship's bell beside the gate brought instant response: "Wait a minute." Then Rachel Gershon appeared, fiftyish and stocky in a stained sweatsuit. Meaty, weather-beaten face with sharp green redhead's eyes. The hair itself now a carrot and cabbage salad of orange and grey, pulled back and tied like George Washington's.

"Ms. Gershon?"

With a look designed for process servers: "Yes?"

"My name's Winston. I wonder if you could tell me where to find Lee Tolman."

"Nope." She sucked on a cigarette, Bogart-style.

"I see. It's a bit complicated. Could we discuss it a moment?"

A negligent shrug. "Okay, discuss."

"May I come in?" She backed reluctantly away from the open gate and I walked into the little yard.

The fence panels facing the ocean were glass rather than plywood. She resumed the chore I'd interrupted: attacking them with Windex and wadded newsprint.

38

"What do you want with Beverly?"

"Beverly?"

"That's the name I gave her. Lee's her nickname."

"I see. Denise Tolman is thinking of selling the studio and there may be some financial implications for Lee—for Beverly."

"I'll bet. The studio's near-worthless. She won't get much."

"I don't know the financial details."

"I do. I used to run that lot. Roy and I ran it together. It's nothing to me; I got my share in the settlement; but there's not much left for Beverly." She peered at the glass. "Hell. I can't see what I washed and what I didn't." She picked at a spot with a stumpy finger.

"It's on the outside." I walked out the gate and around to the front fence. "Give me the squirter." She handed the Windex bottle over the fence. "Some paper?" She dropped a section over. "Be easier doing both sides at once. Then you can see what's clean."

She looked at me speculatively, then shrugged and flipped her cigarette away. I polished the glass panel.

"Give it back." I handed over the bottle. We stood two feet apart, alternately rubbing the glass and yelling through it. She aimed the bottle at my face and a blue splash spattered the glass. Disconcerting to be fired upon.

"Ms. Gershon, don't you know where Beverly is—or don't you want to tell me?"

"Why should I tell you?"

A moment of polishing to aid reflection. Then I shouted, "To help get her out of trouble."

"You missed a spot."

"Sorry." I scraped at a sea gull dropping.

"That's good. Come on back." I returned to the yard.

"What kind of trouble?"

"I'm not sure. That's why I'm going to find her. I do need your help."

"But why should I help you?"

I gaped a moment, then I couldn't help it: I started laughing.

"What's funny?"

"This conversation: I will if you will. Well *I* will if *you* will."

The sharp green eyes narrowed briefly, then the corners of her mouth reversed angle. "Come on in. I owe you for the window."

The front door opened directly on a square living room with sparse rattan furniture, braided oval rug, and amateur seascapes on off-white walls. She took two glasses from a dish rack in the adjacent kitchen area and polished their rims with a used paper towel.

"I'm having scotch. You?"

"That's fine—with water, please."

She dragged out the drink preparation, perhaps to cover a spot of heavy thinking. I took my scotch and leaned against the breakfast bar.

"Okay, Winston."

"Stoney."

"As in 'broke,' hah? I'm Ritchie; here." She plucked a business card from a dish on the bar: Rachel (Ritchie) Gershon. Tax preparation, real estate, investments—and so forth. Ritual advertisements of the hopeful entrepreneur, like "songs, dances, and snappy patter." Male and female, Ritchie's breed wears polyester, drives a six-year-old Cadillac, and seems to know everything about making money while never quite doing so. This beach-front house must have cost a packet, but something about its sparseness said she only rented.

Ritchie looked at the card I'd offered in exchange: "Doesn't say what you do."

"I'm a film director." Oh yes, and the guy who sprays lane markers on freeways is a painter. "Well to be honest, I've done a few commercials."

Her green stare softened slightly. "You said Lee's in trouble?"

"I don't know that. So far, it's just a feeling. Lee left home about eight months back; got some kind of job with a religious organization. Then they let her go for some reason. She stayed with friends in Hollywood until about two weeks ago, then dropped out of sight."

"Two weeks isn't that long."

"True, but I get the impression that Lee's a bit, well, could I say *unworldly*?"

"Beverly isn't crazy."

"Oh I didn't mean that. It's just that she appears vulnerable."

Ritchie swallowed a gulp of scotch big enough to wash in. "You'd be surprised. What's all this about the studio?"

This small, solid, grumpy woman deserved the truth—but not about the film. Ritchie's feeling for Lee seemed to be affection mixed with a sort of puzzled pride. I couldn't jeopardize it with tales of dirty movies.

I compromised: "Denise Tolman is trying to sell the studio. I don't honestly know whether that affects Lee. I'm doing some legwork for Denise because things are slow right now." One of Ritchie's sharp glances. "As usual, in my case."

She smiled her understanding. "Ah, the dear old Industry. I guess I'm well out of it." But remembering, she looked wistful, then concealed her expression behind her glass of scotch. She engulfed another three ounces and set the glass down.

"All right. I'll tell you what I know. Lee worked for a Burbank preacher named Isiah Hammond for about six months after she left home. Then—well she *says* she quit, but I think he fired her."

"You've seen her, then?"

"About two weeks ago." The flat mouth wrinkled briefly. "An average visit: she stayed about an hour. Said she was thinking of something new—another religion or guru or some damn thing. She gets saved about every six months. But she didn't say what or where." With dignity: "We really aren't that close."

"Did she ask for money?"

"No, she *gave* me some: two hundred dollars. Repaid an old loan. Hell, I didn't want it, but she insisted."

"Know where it came from?" Ritchie shrugged. "But I heard Lee was broke."

"She gave me cash and there was more in her wallet." Ritchie's face changed. "Then she left again and that was that." She was still reducing her scotch with the negligent regularity of an accomplished drinker.

"Can you tell me anything else?"

"Not much. Beverly's real hard to get close to. She lives inside herself; always has. When she was just a little kid, she used to sit in a big maple rocker we had. She'd stay there for hours, just rocking and humming and rocking."

"Have you any pictures of her?" I hoped to find a contrast to the doleful film I'd studied.

She walked into the bedroom, lightly for such a chunky woman. Rummaging sounds and the audible monologue of a solitary person: "Now where the hell? . . . No, no, I thought I put it . . . wait a minute: yeah." She carried in a cheap drugstore photo album, placed it between us on the breakfast bar, jammed a pair of outsized glasses on her nose, and thumbed the black pages.

"Years ago I started saving Beverly's school pictures. Even after the divorce, she sent one every year." Finding the page, she revolved the book so I could see it.

Thirteen small color prints identified in a strong, sloppy hand: *kindergarten, first grade, second grade*—all the way through high school. The color improved over the years and the seamless paper backings went from blue to chocolate to mottled tan to blue again. The blouses matured along with their wearer and the carrot hair evolved from childish tousle to modish cut. Braces appeared and then for two years more, Lee smiled close-mouthed, until they came off again.

But the face: at five and six and seven, just another little redhead girl. Then an eerie transformation began: from year to year, the green eyes grew larger, the smile more distant, the skin—even in fading Ektacolor—more translucent, so that the backlighting almost seemed to penetrate the body. It was like looking at frames of a film effect: the actress was slowly dissolving out of the shot.

"She seems frail."

Ritchie replenished her scotch with offhand accuracy. "No, that's just her expression. She's really kind of horsey."

Something funny about that. What?

"You said Lee *sent* the later pictures. Didn't she visit?"

"Not often. The divorce wasn't friendly and I had to trade some rights for cash." Growing truculence, abetted by scotch. "Had to. No job. Never worked, except for Roy. I always did the studio books so I learned accounting—not CPA stuff but enough to find work." Sudden awareness of her stained sweatsuit and bare feet. "I do okay."

I looked again at the ranks of grave girls, all training their green eyes on me. I closed the album.

"What's the matter with you, Stoney?"

This is the word of the Lord, which He spake by His servant Elijah the Tishbite, saying, "In the portion of Jezreel shall dogs eat the flesh of Jezebel . . ."

"I have to find her. Hammond's church, I think."

"Don't go blundering in." Ritchie started a third large scotch, again using the time to come to a decision. "Beverly didn't just work there; she was Hammond's mistress."

"What?"

"Well, whatever they call it now. But that's what she was. She told me."

"That doesn't fit Lee." *Or does it?*

"Just happened, I guess. She got the job through the studio. Hammond shoots religious pictures there. I suppose one thing led to another."

"With a minister?"

"He wouldn't be the first one. I think he got tired of her and that's how she came by the money. Hammond paid her for services rendered and laid her off." A snort. "So to speak."

"Did Lee tell you this?"

"Just a guess. She never talks much—at least to me."

"But she did say she was involved with Hammond?"

"I had the feeling she needed to talk about it. But I guess I don't handle the mother thing very well—outa practice. She told me the main parts and then, well, kinda petered out." The fleshy face was sagging now and the green eyes weren't quite as sharp.

"Right." I slid off the bar stool feeling faintly dazed. "I'll find her."

"Call me when you do. I guess I'd like to know."

"I promise."

"And you be careful, hear?"

"I don't think there's any danger."

"I mean about Beverly. She'll get to you. Prob'ly did already. She's good at that." Ritchie inspected her scotch. "But you won't reach her. Nobody does."

Aiming the Rabbit down Conejo Grade, in conversation with another imaginary companion. This time it was Sherlock Holmes, who had temporarily taken over the driving.

"Where are we now, Holmes?"

"On Route 101 to Los Angeles. My *dear* Winston, do keep alert," he added in a testy tone reminiscent of Basil Rathbone.

"Sorry, Holmes; guess I nodded off. Oh yes, we're passing Thousand Oaks."

"Precisely ninety trees, by my count, Winston. A typical example of California's hopeful exaggeration."

"Right; but Holmes, what do you make of this case?"

"Suspicious contradictions, my dear fellow."

"Meaning?"

"Mrs. Tolman is afraid Isiah Hammond will see her stepdaughter's unmentionable film. But the girl turns out to be the reverend gentleman's, ah, favorite, so one wonders how much the film would disturb him."

"That *is* a thought."

"Adroit of you to recognize one." Holmes avoided a lumbering truck with languid ease. "Moreover, Denise Tolman is attempting to sell her studio. If this be so, why should she care to retain the church's business?"

"You're right; it doesn't make sense."

"On the contrary, Winston, it makes perfect sense. We have only to discover *how*. You will have noted her strange behavior on the telephone."

"That worries me. Perhaps I should go out there tonight."

"I think not. Her tone suggested anger and distress, but no danger."

"Tomorrow then."

Holmes swerved the Rabbit around a trudging camper van. "Take care, Winston: you're making excuses to visit the woman."

"Now don't *you* start on me. What about Lee Tolman?"

"The child had a bit of money—we know that—and an apparent affinity for religions of dubious orthodoxy, or so her mother implied." Holmes filled and lit his calabash reflectively, steering with his knees.

"Do you think *she's* in danger?"

"Rather more than that, Winston," he replied gravely; "I shouldn't be surprised if she turned up dead."

"*Dead?*"

My shout vaporized Holmes and left me in my empty little car, staring past the sick green dashboard glow at the empty road.

Why did he say "dead"?

5

Gazing, half awake, at Sally's terry cloth back as she beat a pan of eggs into submission. Sally cooks with her whole body and her short robe was working loose around her swinging stern.

Scrub jays squabbling outside the French doors; sunshine and bacon smell filling the warm kitchen; even the newspaper's ration of doom was reassuringly familiar. In fact, it was almost *too* good. The domestic clichés seemed orchestrated, like a scene in a TV commercial. Any minute now, Rover would shamble in with his bowl in his mouth, begging for breakfast.

Sally turned to deliver coffee and sure enough, the robe had quit trying to embrace her exuberance. She dispensed eggs offhandedly, deposited the skillet, and only then rebelted the robe. As if we were a long-married couple.

Grouch, mumble, grump.

Sally looked up from the sports pages. "You're really Mr. Warmth this morning."

"Not your fault, Sally."

She returned to the paper. Pause; fade up ticking clock effect. At length: "What's wrong?"

"I'm not really sure."

"Something about the girl?"

"There's nothing about a girl."

"Don't be crabby; I said *the* girl—the one in the film."

"Hmp."

"You need more coffee to grease your brain. I know you." She reached to refill my cup.

"Do you ever wear clothes?"

"Yep, starting this minute. I have to be at the office at nine." She strode off to the bedroom, shucking her robe as she went.

Sally reappeared two cups later in full business battle dress: flowing blouse and suit cut for success.

"Ready to say what's bothering you?"

Might as well: "You act as if we've been married for years."

Sally blinked at this typical male non sequitur. "How so?"

"The comfortable routine. The . . . I don't know . . . matter-of-factness."

"Is that a word?"

"Don't get me wrong: I *like* bourgeois domesticity. But it usually starts with bourgeois *marriage*."

"Okay, I'll play the tape again. I enjoy my work. I like making a thousand dollars a week. And I depend on nobody. There's no way I'll risk losing all that."

"I'm not asking you to."

"That's what my husband said—and he meant it as sincerely as you do. But somehow, equality never works out. Somebody has to be second."

"I don't believe that."

"I know, but it's true." Sally found her attaché case, checked its contents briskly, and started for the door. "Fact is, I kind of love you. Why does it have to be official?"

Exit Sally, screen-left.

Out to Pasadena in the dry September sunshine, pining for remembered English thunderheads to relieve this blue, boring sky. The San Rafael area was deserted except for pickup trucks bristling with rakes and mowers. Behind the estate walls, it was gardener's day. Mostly Mexicans, now that the Orientals are all preoccupied with medical school and systems engineering. Something to be said for California mobility: in twenty years, the Mexicans will run things, in their turn.

I found Denise in her pool, thrashing out clumsy laps. I waited for three round trips, then grabbed a long-handled pool brush and lowered it in front of her like a parking gate.

"Oh, Stoney. I didn't see you." She swam to the side of the pool and hung on to the lip. "Uh, go on in the kitchen, will you? I'm getting right out."

"That's okay."

She looked at me with something like annoyance, then heaved herself up onto the deck, rotated awkwardly on her arms, and plopped onto the concrete. "Give me that towel, will you?" I handed her about fifteen square feet of heavy terry cloth, which she held in front of her as she rose. "This isn't my company swimsuit."

She was wearing a faded bikini outgrown twenty pounds ago. "Looks fine to me."

She studied my face, then accepted my compliment and smiled. "Let's go in the kitchen." She picked her way on tiptoe along the garden stepping-stones with elbows bent and arms raised like a schoolgirl running. I walked in her small, wet footprints.

"Now: how about some coffee? Or maybe a drink? A screwdriver? Why not?" Without waiting for my answer, Denise darted around the kitchen fetching glasses, vodka, orange juice in a cut glass pitcher.

"A bit early for me."

"Oh, sin a little." She flashed a nervous smile, caught halfway between humor and seductiveness. A glass went *ting* when she hit its rim with the pitcher.

"Denise, you know why I'm here."

She nodded, her nervousness increasing. "Last night; your call."

"Can you tell me what was wrong?"

She drank half her glass. "Nothing—really. Things just sort of got to me. I was, well, down a little."

"But nothing specific?"

She shook her head and drained the rest of her glass.

I tried a new direction: "If you sell your lot, why do you need to keep the church's business?"

She started absently on my glass, which she had forgotten to give me. A silence while she drank, then: "Well, I guess the same reason I want to keep my staff there. Harry said a buyer'd want to see that the studio had regular customers. And Hammond's my only one."

"Hummel seems to be giving you a lot of advice."

Defensively: "Something wrong with that?"

"I don't mean to intrude, but Harry's not exactly a world-class businessman "

Denise sipped and sighed. "I think maybe you're right. But we once were . . . anyway, he's all the advice I've got, now." She finished my drink.

"Well, I'm no expert, but you *are* paying me to help."

"I hoped you could, Stoney, but I don't know. . . ."

"Last night, you said you were afraid to tell me something. Why was that?"

A long, indecisive look, then: "They said I'm not supposed to."

"Who, the people who want money for the tape? What did they say?"

"I can't . . ." She looked uncertain, then thought of something: "But they didn't say I couldn't *show* you. Come on." Denise rose and led the way into the hall and up the stairs. "I put it away for safekeeping."

Halfway up the stairs, she wobbled and leaned back, hanging on to the bannister. I put an arm around her waist.

"Hoo, your hand's cold. What's happening?"

"Two screwdrivers in five minutes. You have any breakfast?" She shook her head. "No wonder. Come on."

I helped her the rest of the way. In the upper hallway I turned her loose, and she walked unsteadily into a bedroom. I followed her into a blue-green riot of wallpaper, bedspread, and drapery flowers that threatened to overgrow maple dressers and a king-sized colonial bed. She rummaged in a drawer.

"This came in the mail yesterday."

Plain bond paper with words penciled in an unformed but feminine script:

> *If you want to keep your studio safe,*
> *don't tell anybody about the tape.*
> *We will contact you about the money.*

"You see why I'm afraid to tell you? What if they do something to my studio? It's all I own."

"What could they do to a studio?"

"I don't know, but I can't take a chance. You have to forget the whole thing, Stoney."

"Sit down, Denise. Let's think about this." We plopped on the bed. "Do you recognize the handwriting?"

She leaned over to look at the paper and her thigh pressed against my jeans. "No. I don't think it's Lee's. I don't know what to do."

"Take it easy. Look, Lee is still the key. If I find her, I'll learn who made that tape."

"But if they know you're looking. . . ."

"No need to know. You can say I'm doing something else."

"What?"

"Say—well, say I'm a consultant you've hired to advise you on . . . on what? On renovating your studio."

"But I'm trying to sell it."

"Right, but if people think you're fixing it up, it'll kill any rumors that you're getting rid of it."

Denise trained an ardent, unfocused stare. "Will it work?"

"I think so."

"Oh, that would be wonderful!" And she draped an arm across my shoulder. "Stoney, you're a marvel." The expression on her face, six inches away, was unmistakable and I felt a slight impulse to respond. Besides, I liked having a woman call me a marvel.

Oh yes, and fetch my slippers and answer to *come*, *sit*, and *heel*.

"Denise, sitting on this bed with you is exciting, but there's two problems. First, you just had six ounces of vodka on an empty stomach."

Resentfully: "What's the other?"

I delivered it with a smile, to take the edge off: "You smell like chlorine." Before she could react, I stood up. "Now I have to see Isiah Hammond."

The subject change distracted her. "What for?"

"To learn where Lee went. I'll tell him I'm a consultant directing your studio renovation, so I need to find out his production needs. After all, he's your most important customer."

"But I've never personally talked to him."

"Then have Pepe call and get me an appointment."

"I'll have to give a reason."

"Tell Pepe the same story: I'm a consultant. Phone him right now; maybe I can get an appointment today."

"Okay. Just let me put some clothes on." She smiled uncertainly, then picked up the bedside phone.

Toiling up the Hollywood Freeway in my geriatric Rabbit, en route to Tolman Studios, I began to wonder if the late Roy Tolman was drawn to boozers. Ritchie last night and now Denise this morning; both of them packing it away.

Off at Santa Monica Boulevard, then left, past shabby ranks of porno shops: *Le Sexe Boutique, Arnold's Adult World*. On an impulse, I pulled over and parked. Hm: this area must have the last nickel meters in town.

The shop was a blowsy storefront between a three-stool diner and a shabby store displaying hideous sofas on the sidewalk. Greasy curtains screened the shop interior from delicate pedestrians, one of whom had nonetheless heaved a rock at the front window. Its plywood-backed remnants said:

BOOKS ND MAGAZ
NO ONE UND   21
ADMITT

Inside, the store was split in half. The left-hand doorway opened on a labyrinth of closed booths, each supplied with two coin-operated projectors. Large signs forbade multiple booth occupants and self-abuse, and a sort of menu described each film.

Several men lurked among the booths: a seedy geezer, a shabby adolescent, and a fugitive from an Elks Club lunch.

The other side bulged with films and tapes, books and magazines, plastic appliances, and elixirs guaranteeing priapic results. The high-racked magazines offered blacks, orientals, Lolitas, amazons in rubber knickers, obese matrons, and transsexuals with contradictory fixtures. Overall, a depressing reflection of the joyless souls driven to this refuge of fixed smiles and flaunted paper parts. Must be thousands of them hiding out there, judging from the size of the stock.

The skinny clerk stood on a high platform behind a counter, where he could enforce the sign reading *Shoplifters Will Be Prosecuted!* I grabbed a magazine at random and sidled forward, grateful that the plywood window screened me from the street.

"Six-forty, with the tax." The clerk changed my ten and bagged the purchase deftly, then produced a glossy film box. "Here's a brand new film: *Bazoom Orgy.* A guy and five chicks." The satyr on the box photo was apparently romping with a small herd of Guernseys. "Need a projector? We gotta special. Everything's goin' to tape nowadays."

"No, I have a setup. Matter of fact, I make my own— you know, with friends?"

"Yeah? You sell 'em?"

"Don't know how; who to see; that kind of thing."

"It's tough nowadays. Use to be, an innapendent could sell anything, but now it's all perfessional."

"Lots of money in it."

"My boss makes his own line: *Danish Party Films*. He's got outlets in four states."

"They come from Denmark?"

"Hell no; makes 'em right here. Gotta lab out in the Valley and a deal with a studio."

"What's your boss' name? Maybe I could interest him."

"He don't give it out. Keeps a low profile, right? Besides, like I said, he makes his own."

"He must be big. Most people don't shoot in studios."

"Also, he's gotta deal with the manager."

"Hey, that sounds like Pepe Delgado. He told me all about it. Never saw your boss there, though. I thought Pepe ran it."

"'Swhat you're suppose to think." A knowing nod· "Low profile, right?" Then to business: "Come back next week. We're getting some new *San Francisco Specials*. Real dynamite."

"Your boss make them?"

"Nah, that kind he won't touch. You know: animals and stuff. I mean, you gotta draw the line."

"How true."

As I stepped out onto the sidewalk, a very pregnant Mexican woman glanced at me in passing. Avoiding her look, I scuttled back to the Rabbit, imagining the eyes of the neighborhood on my back.

As I closed the car door, I furtively dropped the bagged magazine into the street. The law doesn't care if I buy pornography, but they're very severe about littering.

I lurched along Santa Monica toward Tolman Studios, where Mr. Low Profile shoots his little epics. Check that one out.

I was delayed at Wilton Place by a bag lady, whose shopping cart self-destructed in the intersection. All traffic stopped dead while she retrieved and stowed her sacks, but nobody yelled or blew a horn. Oblivious, she made her glacial way to the opposite curb, as one traffic lane after another revved, roared, and started behind her.

Entering the musty studio lobby, I greeted Gladys Dempal: part-time receptionist, bookkeeper, and all-purpose office top sergeant.

"Hey, Gladys!"

"Stoney!" She pulled horn-rims off her blunt nose, spread her stubby arms, and rose for a ritual buss on the cheek.

"Mmmmuhh!" At five feet even, Gladys resembles a fireplug in a gray wig. "What're you doing here, Stoney? Don't tell me we're going to get some business?"

"I thought that church had you all booked up, Gladys."

"Would it were so, dearie, but they're falling off month by month. We're dark more'n half the time now. Mornings I don't even come in."

"I know. Leaving things to Pepe?"

She snorted, grinning. "I run the front half and he runs the back. We stay clear of each other."

"Pepe here?"

"I guess. He doesn't tell me what he's doing."

I started for the inner door. "All right, I'll hunt him up."

"You never said why you're here today?"

"Oh, just keeping in touch."

Gladys had been in radio, decades back. Now she dropped into "Mrs. Nussbaum": "So dun't be such a stren-jair."

I smiled as I let myself into the studio corridor.

Today, Pepe favored the world with a fawn-colored shirt—unbuttoned to reveal gold neck chains—burgundy pants, and loafers the color of uncooked sausage. After the usual ritual of finishing more pressing business, he responded predictably to my request.

"If we are fixing up the studio, why do I not know this, eh?"

I shrugged.

"And if Mrs. Tolman wants to interview the church about this thing, why am *I* not doing it?"

"Denise's orders, as you know, Pepe."

Silence while his wizened face grew even more prune-like. Then: "Hammond won't see you."

"Why not?"

"He does not handle the film production."

"Who does?"

"I think his name is Nahan."

"You think?"

"He is the church business manager. I think. I am not sure."

"Get me an appointment with Nahan. What's his full name?"

"Wilton M. Nahan."

"You think. Then call him." Pepe sat there. "Pepe, did Denise phone you this morning?" Glum nod. "And did she tell you what to do?" Another nod. "Then shall we do it?"

Finally he called Nahan, relaying my made-up story with all the conviction of a recorded phone message. It worked though: he got me an appointment for one PM.

Pepe hung up, looking truculent. "First, I hear Mrs. Tolman is selling the studio. Then I hear she is fixing it up. But no one is telling me these things. I am only the manager, of course, but may one inquire? . . ."

"One may inquire of Mrs. Tolman, Pepe. Like you, I only work here."

"Correction, my good friend: you do not work *here*. And I do not like you around."

"Then buy the lot and summarily evict me. Until then, Pepe, hasta la vista."

Turning to pull his door closed behind me, I saw Pepe at his desk, his expression a mixture of anger and fear.

I strolled furtively down the echoing hallway toward the soundstage door, heaved it open and slipped through. No real reason for stealth, but the empty studio felt spooky somehow, as if I were searching someone's vacant house.

I was hoping to find some traces of Mr. Low Profile's operation. Dim work light from ceiling fixtures thirty feet above, half-blocked by suspended boardwalks festooned with two- to ten-thousand watt lights. Hammond's desert tent set was replaced with a hospital room: bed, bell cord, metal table. The big fresnel-faced lights were aimed to hit this set, so it had been used.

Not much else about: director's chairs, a wooden prop table, dented wastebasket. I snooped through the dusty, twilit stage, behind the plywood flats, in the corners. Nothing. Even the cloth pocket on the script girl's chair arm was empty.

The wastebasket was full of white cloth tapes stripped from a camera slate. Pulling them apart, I deciphered the markings: separate numbers and letters to make up shot identifications. Nothing to indicate the production company or director. Wait, a title: #31; *Night Nurse Nooky.*

Got it.

I pocketed the tape as the stage door opened and a woman entered. In the dim light, it took a moment to recognize Peeper Martin. The jeans and Kabuki makeup were the same, but her mood today ran to Orphan Annie wig and green see-through blouse.

"Winston?"

"Hi, Peeper."

"What're you doing in here?"

"Snooping around. What are *you* doing?"

She stepped forward hesitantly. "I saw you go in. What're you snooping for?"

"Where are your vitamins?"

"Aw, I don't do that all the time. It's like a—avocation, right?" She looked pleased that she'd remembered the word.

"Right. Did you want to talk to me?"

She clacked over to the hospital bed, then turned self-consciously and sat down. I took a chair.

"Hey, I don't wanna yell." She patted the bed beside her and I changed seats as requested. I seemed to be sitting on a lot of beds today.

"I was thinking, you know, about Lee and all? I mean the studio thing. Well, I probly might be able to help you find her." She gazed reflectively down through the gauzy blouse at her small, sloping breasts. They reminded me of scenery foothills, softened by a scrim.

"She wasn't at Candy Wishbourne's."

"Yeah, well, I knew that. The thing is, I didn't really want to tell you. I mean, it's gotta be worth it—oh, worth it to Lee, right? Not me, I mean. You know, maybe she wants to stay lost." Another pause while her thoughts trudged on. "But like I said before, if she's got something coming to her, well, it's only, well, fair."

"Do you really know where Lee is, Peeper?"

She swung her legs up on the bed and lay back. "Maybe."

"I see. What do you want me to say before you decide to tell me?"

Groping at the side of the bed, she found the electric control and raised the head and foot. I ended up sitting in a shallow valley with Peeper draped behind me.

"What do you want me to tell you, Peeper?"

"I dunno. People tell you anything you wanna hear, right? But I can catch the vibes. I'm sensitive."

"Where do you want me to start?"

"Just tell me what's coming down. Are they gonna sell the lot? I mean, Pepe's all steamed."

I decided to play my fish a bit: "Gee, Peeper, I don't know; that's kind of confidential."

Peeper shifted until her hip pressed against the small of my back. "Hey, I'm use to confidential. I'm like a doctor, remember?"

I nodded, pretending to consider this, then: "Well, Denise Tolman's going to sell the studio and that means some money for Lee."

"How soon?"

"Whenever she finds a buyer, I guess. Only, there's a problem."

I paused long enough to make Peeper prompt me: "Yeah?"

"Okay, here's the problem, but can I trust you to keep it quiet?" She pushed her hip against me harder. "You won't believe this, but somebody's making porno movies in this studio."

Peeper's reaction was just a hair late: "Wow! Here?" She sat up and leaned toward me.

"On this very stage. I found out some other things too."

"Like what?"

"I don't think I should talk about them."

Peeper looked uncertain, then something occurred to her. "Hey, you think they used this bed? That's a great idea—this electric bed? Look what you could do!"

She lay back, knees spread wide in the air, legs doubled under her so that her high-heeled boots almost touched her buttocks. "Okay, roll it!" Peeper pushed the button on the bed control. As the head of the bed reclined, she arched her pelvis and reached her hands toward me between her thighs, palms up, as if proffering a melon.

"Wanna play?"

When I made no response, she dropped the act and sat up, scowling. "You don't think that's a turn-on."

"It's very stimulating."

"You don't act like it."

I waved an arm around the stage: "I guess it's the atmosphere."

"Yeh, I guess. Hey, I just remembered: you told Pepe you were gonna help fix up the lot. That's not selling it. So which is it?"

"You and Pepe seem to talk a lot."

"What's that suppose to mean?"

"What does Pepe have to do with these porno films?"

"How should I know? Boy, you're really something else." She jumped off the bed and hustled toward the door.

"I thought you wanted to help Lee."

"I thought *you* did, but you're just working for that fat bitch. You think I'm gonna help *her*?" Peeper timed the line to take her to the door. She yanked it open and disappeared up the hall.

I followed quickly, expecting Peeper to head upstairs toward Pepe's office. Instead, she turned left, toward Gladys Dempal up front. I came into the lobby just as Peeper raced out the front door.

I watched her hike across the parking lot, then turned to Gladys, acting casual. "Say, did Pepe go out?"

"About ten minutes ago. You miss him?"

"No, we had a nice chat. Listen, Gladys, I might have some business for you after all. Harry Hummel needs some editing space. I wondered if you had any rooms open."

"But of course."

"I'd like to check out the equipment. Got a key?"

She fished a key from her top desk drawer. "Here, this submaster fits all the cutting rooms. I'm going to lunch, so just put it back when you're through."

I thanked her and headed back into the studio.

With everybody gone, I should have owned the place, but I still felt the grey, oppressive silence. I headed down the grimy, half-lit hall, up the creaking stairs, and along the hallway to the left, toward the cutting rooms at the back of the building.

The first two rooms were empty and full of dust. A hand-lettered sign on the third door: Pisces Productions. I knocked softly to make sure. No answer. Inside, the usual chaos of a working editing room. Trim bin full of 35mm film. I held a length up to the light to find a slate: "Hartley's Instant Coffee." A commercial.

The fourth room was similar, but the film was 16mm. Harder to see this smaller gauge. Pulling a shot from the bin, I snapped open the green Moviola head, and laid the film in the chrome channel. Head down, switch on, hit the foot pedal.

The slate said "Night Nurse Nooky" and the footage showed a couple grappling on a hospital bed. The male was turbaned by an unconvincing bandage and the female was stripped to garterbelt, white stockings, and sturdy nurse's shoes—a nice touch of authenticity.

Check the bench: the usual synchronizer, grease pencils, rack full of empty reels. No paperwork or anything else to identify the editor.

Cracking the door, I scanned the empty hall and sidled out.

A quick look into the last room revealed hundreds of dusty silver film cans stored on metal racks. Nothing there.

Better get back.

I headed through the empty lobby to drop the key in Gladys' desk drawer. Sudden clatter of the telephone. Letting it ring, I worked the snap lock on the front door and eased out into the parking lot. Just time to get out to Burbank for my one o'clock appointment with Wilton M. Nahan.

6

BUT FIRST A QUICK TRIP HOME TO CONSULT MY WARDROBE
department. Let's see: my professor costume, I think: cor-
duroy jacket, tan shirt and slacks, and penny loafers. Better
submit to a tic; Nahan *was* a business manager. And for the
final touch, a plastic nerd pack full of pens in the shirt
pocket.

Not bad.

I guess if I wanted acting jobs, I would have to cast
myself.

Then up over Cahuenga Pass and down again into the
San Fernando Valley toward Burbank and the Reverend
Hammond's Universal Church. "The Valley" should be off-
limits to tourists. For some reason, it's all they recall about
Southern California: cookie cutter houses giving way to vast
apartments done up as Polynesian compounds. Concrete
office blocks strung along a few boulevards like cottonwood
trees marking an underground stream. Endless stucco fac-
tories baking in the desert glare. Everything squat, drab,
and unfocused. Textbook sprawl.

Hammond's domain looked like any other factory: no
visible church; just a long, scabby building with a cross on
one wall. A billboard proclaimed:

WATCH ISIAH HAMMOND'S
DAY OF THE LORD
WEEK NIGHTS AT EIGHT ON CHANNEL 51

in changeable marquee letters. The asphalt parking lot re-
served eight stalls for handicapped drivers—faith healing

candidates, perhaps. Double doors to the left labeled "Studio"; single door to the right marked "Office."

Behind the seedy facade, the foyer was a shock: all high tech furnishings and hot fabrics and everywhere, the symbol of corporate bravery: op art prints. Beyond, sleek bureaucrats carried papers through a maze of office dividers. It looked like IBM headquarters.

The receptionist presided over a switchboard worthy of a war room—taking, switching, holding calls; attacking fifty buttons with candy apple nails. She phoned ahead on my behalf, then sent me fifty yards along a hallway.

Nahan's walnut bunker was guarded by a prison matron dressed in iron gray, with hair and complexion to match.

"Mr. Nahan will see you if he's free."

"I have an appointment."

Her silence signaled what she thought of that.

I sat in a chair designed to mortify the flesh and hobnobbed with the plutocrats in *Business Week* while she communed with the screen of her word processor.

I'd absorbed a lengthy exegesis of offshore tax shelters before the Matron's phone beeped.

"Mr. Nahan will give you a few minutes now."

I walked toward his office door, pulling on the mantle of business consultant.

No one emerged as I entered his office and there was no other door. Wilton Nahan had simply kept me waiting. He and Pepe were two of a kind.

No greeting: "Sit down, Mr. . . ." He trained silver-rimmed bifocals on his desk appointment book. ". . . Winston."

"Mr. Nahan, I'm doing some consulting for Denise Tolman. She owns the studio where your church makes its films."

"I am aware of that. Why is she consulting you?" His tone implied that I was a dubious source of advice on any subject.

"Our firm is helping her plan a modernization project. Before she makes a substantial investment in new equipment, she wants to find out what her most important customers might need. She said you were the most knowledgeable person."

Nahan nodded his silver head, as if my compliment were a simple statement of fact.

"But she didn't explain your responsibilities here at the church."

"They are quite complex." Nahan removed his glasses and held them as if posing for his picture in *Fortune*. "Of course, you know I am the Executive Vice President and General Manager of the Universal Church."

My nod agreed that *everyone* knew that.

"In that capacity, I function as Executive Producer of all media projects, including inspirational and instructional films."

"But you're not the line producer."

"Let's just say I keep a very close eye on production."

"Fine, then to see what your needs might be, could we discuss your future plans?"

"I'm afraid you will find them disappointing. We are phasing out film production."

"You won't be providing any more films to churches?"

"I didn't say that." He smiled thinly, as if he'd just won a little game. "I said we are phasing out *film*. We are converting to tape. We have a state of the art video facility here, so producing elsewhere isn't cost-effective."

"Have you mentioned this to Mrs. Tolman?"

"I believe our intentions are clear." He consulted an oversize silver clock on his desk. "I'm due at the studio now, so if there is nothing more to discuss. . . ."

Thinking fast, then: "Mrs. Tolman's planning to offer tape-to-film transfer. Do you record on two-inch, one-inch, or three-quarter?"

Nahan looked distinctly sour at being caught without an answer. "I don't concern myself with technicalities."

"To find out then, could I come look at your setup?"

He paused, as if trying to think of a reason for refusing, then shrugged. "I suppose so, but I won't have time to talk. I'll be engaged with Reverend Hammond." Standing up, Nahan twitched his vest into perfect alignment and added a silver Cross pen to two others standing at attention in his pocket. As he crossed to the door, I realized that his prissy delivery was misleading. Behind the desk, he'd seemed a small, almost elderly man. But Nahan was a well-muscled six-footer in his late forties. He opened the door and walked out, leaving me to trail behind.

As we left, the Matron was eyeing an emerging print-out with grim vigilance, as if fearing that the computer was prone to frivolity. "A call for you, Mr. Nahan." She proffered a slip of pink paper, which Nahan studied impassively.

"When was this?"

"Thirty minutes ago." The slightest tart edge crept in: "I wrote down the time, as always. She'd like you to return the call."

Nahan put her back in her place. "You wrote that down too. As always." He pocketed the slip and walked out, again leaving me to trail behind.

Nahan paced off the distance to the studio as if he'd previously counted the steps and would allow the journey no more and no less. I caught him up, then matched his stride, and we marched along together, an army of two.

"By the way, Denise Tolman sends her regards." He nodded. "I guess you know her daughter, Lee, too." He flicked a glance suggesting that this chitchat was uncalled for.

I persisted: "She works here."

"Worked."

"Oh really? I didn't know she'd quit. I guess I haven't seen Lee for a while. How long ago did she leave?"

"I don't recall."

"Funny, she said she liked it here. I wonder why she left." No reaction. "Did she say?"

"Not to me."

"Do you know what Lee's doing now?"

This time, the look was distinctly cold. "No."

He pulled open the studio door, entered, and strode away in a plain gesture of dismissal. I followed him into the building, pausing just inside the door.

A typical TV studio: six tiers of empty seats wrapping around two walls. Three color cameras on wheeled pedestals, aimed at the lit set by operators in jeans and golf shirts. To the right, a small choir in burgandy robes, watching their leader at an electric organ. Plain table center stage. Pretty makeup girl patting the forehead of an impressive figure sitting casually on the table edge: the Reverend Isiah Hammond.

Thick chest and shoulders under a cream shirt. Strong, big-nosed face tanned by sun or makeup, below the wavy brown pompadour of a used-car salesman. The girl helped him into his sober blue suit coat. His large paw gave her shoulder more than just a friendly squeeze and his appreciative blue eyes followed her off the set.

The speaker on the wall erupted: "All set, Reverend?" Hammond waved up at the director, invisible in the glass-fronted booth. The disembodied voice boomed, "Okay, let's make one."

The color monitor showed a slate, then the picture shifted to the choir, on camera two.

The floor manager drawled, "We're rolling," and cued the choir:

> *My Savior appeared at the river,*
> *In the shade of an old willow tree-e-e,*
> *And I looked on the face*
> *Of the Lord of the race,*
> *My Savior who suffered for me!*

The choir dipped under, humming another stanza. A little red dome glowed on camera one and Hammond shifted subtly.

"My dear brothers and sisters in Jesus Christ, consider what our Lord meant when He said 'Render unto God the things that are God's.'" The voice a fruity, folksy drawl; clear, level gaze. "My friends, God needs your offerings; needs your pennies, dimes, quarters, an' dollars. He needs them to heal the sick; He needs them to comfort the afflicted; He needs them to clothe the naked. An' He needs them to spread His Divine Word!"

The old-time cadences rolled. Half-hidden by camera one, the real Hammond was motionless and uncompelling. But the video image on the floor monitor was hypnotic. The massive head loomed; the deep eyes stared out, benign and sorrowful; and the rumbling voice drawled on: "Send your dollars, dear brothers and sisters; send 'em to me; send 'em now. Dig deep, dear friends, for Jesus!"

No oratory here, no Bryan bouncing if off the bleachers. Hammond pitched it for the microphone like a radio announcer. A media professional.

"I will bless you, my friends, an' the Lord will bless you, an' all the pore, lost souls who hear His Word will bless you, an' your offering will return unto you a thousandfold."

Cue camera two. Choir up full:

> *Well I looked on the face of my Savior,*
> *Who died for my sins long ago-oh,*
> *And the sorrow writ there*
> *Was too heavy to bear,*
> *And I felt my poor heart overflow-oh,*
> *I felt my poor heart overflow!*

The monitor showed a PO box address superimposed over the choir. Cut to camera one; hold the super over Hammond; and fade to black.

Cut.

The loudspeaker boomed, "Looking good. Wanna see playback?"

Hammond's nod was far too small to be seen from the booth at the back, but he knew that camera one was still sending his close-up to the director's monitors. Yes, very obviously a pro.

As the floor monitor started the playback, Hammond walked over to watch. He stood beside me, clearly approving his grave but kindly image. When it was over, the speaker erupted again: "Right on the money for timing. How'd you like it?"

"Real fine." Hammond spoke softly, knowing that his tie clip mike was still live. He noticed me. "How 'bout that?"

"Very clean take." In this business, you develop a repertory of meaningless compliments.

"Do I know you?"

"I'm a friend of Lee Tolman."

Blank stare.

"She was your secretary, wasn't she?"

Pause. Then, "Hard to recollect; I got me such a turnover."

"Lee hasn't been heard from in some time. Her mother's worried."

He shook his head, producing an obviously standard phrase, "Lord pertect the children of today."

"Any idea where she might be?"

"I didn't keep track."

"Why did she leave?"

Hammond appraised me, then nodded as if admitting me to his fold. He removed the mike from his tie and draped the cord over the monitor, then looped a pastoral arm around my shoulder. "You're concerned for this child, I can tell. That's real good. Truth is, she had a few little . . . problems. 'Course I tried to counsel her, but it didn't hep much."

"Problems? I don't mean to pry, but . . ."

The sorrowful blue eyes regarded me for fully five seconds, then: "You may not know it, son, but preachers have troubles like psychiatrists or even," (self-deprecatory smile) "movie stars. Young ladies get sorta funny on 'em."

"Crushes."

"Uh-huh. Sometimes they make things up."

"And Lee was doing this about you?"

"She told other gals in the office that we, uh . . ." He broke off with a significant look.

I decided to play it his way: "Oh my!"

"Now don't you be shocked, son. She meant no harm."

"Golly, Reverend, I hope not."

"Not a mite. But you can see I had to nip it in the bud. I offered her a different job, but . . ." He appended an actory shrug.

"I'm sorry she caused you trouble."

Hammond radiated benign concern. "No trouble atall."

Nahan had been hovering nearby. Now, clearly, his ten-second supply of patience was exhausted and he stepped up to us.

"Isiah, the clock is running and you have six more spots to tape."

"It's *my* money." Hammond was suddenly snappish.

"But I dislike spending it on unnecessary overtime."

"I spend it like I want."

"How true." They sounded like a bickering couple. Nahan ignored me, but Hammond glanced in my direction, then made a visible effort to control himself.

He smiled at Nahan. "Okay then, let's get to it." He beamed at me. "Stay an' watch if you want. Make yourself to home."

Nahan jerked his head toward the empty audience seats: "Up there."

But the loudspeaker second-guessed him: "That's lunch, folks. Hey Winston! How's the boy?"

Whoever the director was, he'd recognized me.

Trailing the same director to our lunch table in a typical Valley watering hole: overscale flagstone walls, pin-lit plastic banquettes, droning soft rock Muzak.

Jerry Galiker made a royal progress among the tables: "Hey good to see ya how's it going we gotta take a lunch gimme a call." Jerry's regal indeed at six-four and 260 pounds, with bristling beard and gray curls cascading to his collar from a yarmulke-sized bald crown. He always behaves like a mogul, but in fact, he's a genial whore who started out directing local TV kiddie shows back in the fifties. To this day, he takes what he can get and is seldom paid much over scale. Just like me.

But out here in the shadow of Burbank studios, his friends are all in the same situation, and they play the Industry Game with a touch of dour self-satire.

We slid crabwise into our booth and confronted the ancient waitress, who seemed to be made of beef jerky.

Jerry saluted her: "Hi! You're Helen; you'll be our waitress."

"Wasn't funny the *first* time, Jerry." Obviously, he was a regular.

Elaborate dialogue about the fish special, the soup du jour, the salad dressings; then Jerry ordered a double cheeseburger.

Helen nodded: "The usual."

"Hey Helen, I'd pat your ass, but it might fall off." Helen returned a patient look, collected the giant plastic menus, and plodded off in her micro-miniskirt, a museum piece now seen only on waitresses.

Jerry did a twenty-minute monologue on his dynamite career prospects before I could get to my own agenda, but when his mouth was finally full of cheeseburger, I had at least a fighting chance.

"I thought Hammond broadcast worship services. How come you're taping spots today?"

"Mmmh. Look, he's on three hours a night. That's a lotta air time. So we pretape promos, choir numbers, junk like that."

"But he does hold services?"

Jerry's smile numbered me among the terminally dim. "Hammond's not a preacher; he's a TV evangelist. No church, no congregation, no nothing. He gets his audience

like a game show." Jerry attacked french fries the size of fish
sticks.

"What about the donations people send in?"

"Whaddya think: he socks them away."

"Aren't there laws about that?"

"Well the state got their pee in a froth about him, but
what can they do? He's a legal church."

"What's he use the money for?"

"Bimbos." Helen shambled up with Jerry's third
Michelob. "Biggest ass man I ever saw—and I seen some
big ones."

"As the actress said to the bishop."

"Hm?"

"Ancient British wheeze. Never mind."

"Oh. Well that guy must of founded the Piece of the
Month Club. New 'secretary' every four weeks. That kinda
hobby takes money. You gonna finish that salad?"

"No."

Jerry engulfed it. "Makes a lotta friction between him
and Nahan."

"I noticed."

"Nahan's your classic anal retentive: squeezes the crap
outa the buffalo nickel. Boy do we fight over budget. Good
salad."

"Does Nahan object to spending money on girls?"

"He's afraid about Hammond's reputation. If people
find out what a chaser he is, it won't do much for his image."

"And his image *is* the church."

"You got it. Nahan's scared shitless of the attorney general's office. They'd do anything to prove Hammond's a
phony."

Catching Helen's rheumy eye, I summoned another
beer for Jerry. "What's Nahan's actual role?"

"There, you got me. Personally, I think he's stashing
away more'n Hammond's spending on gash. But Nahan's so
close to the vest, you can't tell. Bring a clean glass, honey."

"I think I know one of Hammond's girls."

"Yeah? Well it's a statistical probability. Which one?"

"Lee Tolman: redheaded kid with a faraway look."

"I know her; she lasted longer than usual. Funny quality about that kid. Want some dessert? I'm gonna have some dessert."

After another ritual consultation, Helen trudged off with an order of chocolate cake, double à la mode.

Jerry drained his glass. "Y'know, Lee was different. I think she really got to Hammond. Since she left, I haven't seen any new stuff around." He carved out a mountain of cake and dispatched it ruminatively.

"When did she leave?"

"Maybe six weeks ago. *If* she left."

"How do you mean?"

"Think about it: the state is sniffing around. If they find out about Hammond's little hobby, it's bye-bye church. On the other hand, maybe Hammond's really hooked on this kid."

"So?"

"So Hammond gets her outa the spotlight—finds some place to stash her. That's what I think."

"But love nests when out fifty years ago."

"There's other places." An idea dawned: "For instance, Hammond's got a boat—a big sucker too. He could put her there."

"Where is it?"

"I'm not supposed to know it exists. Man of God with a hundred-thousand-dollar yacht; doesn't look good."

"To the attorney general."

"And the faithful. But that's where she's at; I'd lay you money."

"Does Nahan know anything about this?"

"That bastard knows everything. *If* she's there, I mean."

"I thought you'd lay money on it."

Jerry turned suddenly cagey, as if realizing that he'd gone too far. "What I mean is, I don't know. It just stands to reason. Hey! I gotta get back."

He looked briefly distressed when I asked for separate checks, and when he saw my seventy-five-cent tip, he upped his to fifty. "Right, well, glad to hear all about what you're doing, Stoney. And listen, keep in touch. I gotta big special coming up and I just might need an assistant director."

The restaurant was mostly empty now, so Jerry gave only two audiences on the way out.

Retracing my route through the hot afternoon back to Hollywood, I was plagued by an odd memory: that hymn Hammond's choir was singing; I knew it from someplace.

I hummed the tune as I risked life and limb at the Highland Avenue off-ramp. The memory surfaced as the Rabbit clattered downhill past the Hollywood Bowl. Turning right on Hollywood, I dredged up the words from way back in my past:

> *Her beauty he hymned to the morning,*
> *Her virtues extolled through the day-ay,*
> *Her praises he sang*
> *As the Angelus rang,*
> *And at Vespers, they jumped in the hay-ay,*
> *At Vespers, they jumped in the hay!*

7

MY FIRST CALLS TO LOCAL YACHT CLUBS HAD BEEN useless, except to polish the Wally Wimple voice I'd assumed for the walk-on role of diffident bookkeeper. Now the fourth call was ringing.

"Reina del Ray Yacht Club."

"Accounting department please."

On hold, then: "This is Sandy Fujita." Soft young voice.

I did my Milquetoast impression: "Um, yes, Miss Fujita? Yes, my name is Wimple—with the Universal Burbank Church Accounting department?"

"Yes?"

"Frankly, I'm in just an awful mess. We were supposed to renew Reverend Hammond's club membership, but I seem to have lost the file. Can you help me?"

"Just a minute; I'll pull *our* file."

On hold again, then: "Mr. Wimple? Yes, I have it. What did you want?"

"Everything, I'm afraid. I'll have to start a whole new file. Such a nuisance. I don't even know the ship's name."

"Boat."

"Hm?"

"They're called 'boats.' Reverend Hammond's is the *Mixed Blessing*. Thirty-six-foot cutter."

"Well, that's a start. Should I know where it's parked or something?"

"Berthed. Dock H."

"Oh dear, that means nothing to me."

"The end of Dock H. Slip 48. Hm: this membership's good for another six months."

"It is? Oh my goodness. Well, we accountants like to keep ahead of things, don't we? Thank you so much, Miss Fujita."

"Not at all."

If I could only live my life by phone, I could change my personality to suit anyone. What a convenience.

Mixed Blessing. Reina del Rey Yacht Club, Dock H, Slip 48. Everything but the zip code.

Exit Wally Wimple screen right. Enter live-aboard marina bum: sockless sneakers, T-shirt and Levis, shapeless cotton cap, and shades. A banner day for character parts.

Then down to the marina and my first stop: a ship chandler to buy a convincing prop. I hunted vainly for something both nautical and cheap—a contradiction in terms—then reluctantly paid for a 200-foot coil of half-inch line.

Parking the Rabbit in a public lot, I hoofed down a street apparently cut through a thicket of black, white, and silver masts. Everybody's rich but me.

The Reina del Rey Yacht Club was Shopping Mall Spanish: raked tile roof and "adobe" walls faked with slumpstone. I crossed a grass divider to an asphalt path that was separated by a chain-link fence from the long dock fingers floating at right angles to the shore.

Ten docks times 48 slips: almost five hundred boats on this side alone: racers, cruisers, trawler yachts, sportfishers—even a high-class houseboat moored out at the end. No one around this close to supper; just the gulls wheeling in the yellow light and the *tink, tink, tink* of sloppy halyards smacking metal masts. The nearest gate said "J," so H was two doors down.

No way to open the gate without a special card-key; I just had to look legitimate and wait my chance. I lounged along with my coil of line, imagining security guards tracking me from behind the smoke glass yacht club windows: "Potential felon loitering with intent, Fred. Check him out." Too fast; take smaller steps; look purposeful. The club doors were still closed. How long until they saw through me?

A tiny figure climbed off a white ketch and struggled up the dock with two blue sail bags. Dock H! Match his pace: slower—no, faster. Speed it up; he was at the gate.

Covering ground in a sort of hasty saunter, I reached the gate as he dropped a bag and turned the handle.

"Here." I held the gate open, trying to look pleasant for this Fellow Yachtsman.

"Thanks." He hoisted the bags and puffed away without a glance. For all he noticed, I could have been wearing prison stripes. I carefully closed the gate—behind me.

Down the steep ramp to the foot of the dock. Slips marked with painted numbers: 2, 4, 6. Slip 48 would be the last one on the right—sorry—starboard side. I ambled out on the dock, looking nowhere special, peripheral vision alert for movement.

Ah, boats. My old Dad and I sailed our twenty-four-foot tub up every estuary on the south coast of England, parking on twin keels when the long British tides left us stranded on the mud. Dear, dead days. Wonder where the old man is now.

At about slip 36, I spotted *Mixed Blessing* up ahead: a racy yellow bow with lots of overhang. Funny, the bow dock lines were untied. The Reverend Hammond couldn't be much of a sailor. She had a modern-looking trunk cabin, its forward face pierced by a big Lexan hatch. Pretty wet, going to windward in a blow. Above the hatch, the staysail boom scraped gently back and forth across the deck. More sloppiness. This skipper wasn't safe past the breakwater, let alone offshore.

I was alongside now, still sizing things up. The stern lines were very short and taut, to keep the bow from smashing the dock ahead. Cockpit lifelines unclipped, as if someone was aboard. Yes, the big canvas tea cosy was off the wheel and lying on the cockpit sole.

And yet the hatch was closed and the mainsail furled and covered. Time for the straightforward approach: "Hello!"

Nothing. "Hey, *Mixed Blessing!*" Silence.

I climbed over the rail and knuckled the hatchboards. No response.

The hatch cover wasn't padlocked, so I slid it back four inches and peered below. A light burned over a chart table to starboard.

"Anybody home?" Long pause, empty except for the rigging clacking away in the background.

Now or never: I pulled out two hatch boards, slipped the cover another foot, and stepped over the remaining board onto the companionway ladder, replacing the boards and hatch cover behind me.

Standard cabin layout: galley to port, table and settee beyond, forward bulkhead walling off the head and V-berths in the bow. All teak-trimmed Formica and plastic cushions, and not a living soul aboard.

Ducking in the scant headroom, I searched the cabin: galley shelves bulging with cans and freeze-dried food packs. Block ice in the ice box only slightly melted—a centerpiece for several frosty wine bottles.

Hanging locker: full of pricey male leisure clothes, none of them too seaworthy.

I opened the louvered head door and risked another light on: fragrant soap the same shape as the tiny oval sink. Party-style paper guest towels with toilet paper to match. Wonder what that does to a marine toilet?

All-in-all, a floating condo, fitted out for weekend booze and bed.

Thump! Freeze! Kill the light; wait . . . listen . . . Nothing. Just my heart and breath and the water chuckling at me through the plastic hull. False alarm.

What else? Charts: they'd tell me whether Hammond actually sailed this plaything. Let's see: no rolled up charts overhead; maybe folded in the chart table drawer. I'd have to move those sail bags to raise its lid.

The navigator's perch was the protruding forward end of a quarter berth running aft like a low, square tunnel under the cockpit seat above. It was hidden under two big bags stenciled STAYSAIL and 150 GENOA. I shifted the smaller bag, then heaved the big jib out of the way, uncovering a pair of feet and sprawling legs.

I froze.

The legs lay still.

I fumbled for the swing-arm chart lamp and aimed it up the long, tight tunnel.

The girl lay on her back, stuffed into the narrow quarter berth, head wrenched unnaturally back so I could see just her chin, bloody cheek, and tangle of bright orange hair. One slack breast spilled out of her green bikini top. It was spattered with drying blood.

With a kind of wooden calm, I inventoried Lee's details, remembered from the tape: slightly knobby feet, slender legs and haunches—the near one dotted with a mole just emerging from the bottom of her suit. The blue-white skin was cold to the touch.

Her feet almost reached the chart table, so I couldn't pull her straight forward. Instead, I bent her knees slightly, grasped her hips, and pulled. She stuck fast, but my slipping fingers hooked the bikini bottom and yanked it down her cold thighs. I couldn't help noting the improbable orange color of her pubic mound. Her pants and thighs were wet: dying or dead, she'd fouled herself.

I'm used to people faking death: exploding squibs and Technicolor blood and then we shoot their close-ups or clean them up for another take. But riddled, hacked, and bloody as they look, they always get up; it isn't real.

Get up, Lee, that's a print. Get *up*, Lee. But the body lay there, pitiful and final.

Save it for later. I'd broken into someone's boat and now I was hovering over a corpse. Time to move.

I crept over to the hatch and stumbled up the ladder, quietly easing the cover so I could pull the boards. Metallic *clink* as the cover shifted a quarter-inch, then stopped. Harder: *Clink!* Back, then *CLINK!* Nothing. The hatch was locked.

Er-er-er-Rhummm! Starter motor, then the diesel firing. Somebody wasn't through with me yet. Light rocking, then movement: we were backing out of the slip. The bow scraped a piling—this somebody was hurried or inept.

Pause.

The transmission ground, clunked, then the boat slid forward again.

We were leaving the marina.

It had to be Reverend Hammond. He had the card key for the gate and the combination to the hatch padlock. The bow dock lines and lifelines were loose when I'd arrived, so he had been there—someplace. He'd locked his main hatch before taking the boat out, so he knew I was down there. Maybe he hadn't recognized me. The hatch was closed, the cabin dim—but maybe he'd seen me coming up the dock.

All very interesting but off the point, which was to *get out*.

Mixed Blessing veered to port—probably into the main channel—then overcorrected, steadied. Engine revs increased. Hammond was understandably nervous. I glanced quickly around the cabin, trying to avoid seeing the sad refuse in the quarter berth. The tiny ports didn't even open—but the skylight hatch? No, I'd pop right out in front of him. Then I remembered the forward hatch, set into the front of the cabin trunk.

I wrenched open the door to the V-berths in the bow. The overhead hatch was now gaping. That's where he'd come from. He must have been below when I hailed the boat. When I opened the main hatch, he'd closed himself in the forward cabin, and while I fumbled around the main cabin, he'd gone out the forward hatch. So I could too.

Then what? Go overboard, if I could do it before he reached me.

I clambered onto the aft end of the port berth and cautiously approached the open hatch to reconnoiter. Good: the forward-facing opening was invisible from the helm—but then the helmsman was invisible to me too. I poked my head out just as we veered wildly again—to port this time—then straightened. An embankment of huge cubical boulders slid by in the dusk: we were heading right down the center of the main channel. Under power like this, we should be to starboard of those buoys, but our reckless speed showed that the helmsman wasn't observing harbor niceties.

New problem: standing on the V-berth, I could just get head and shoulders through the hatch. Hauling up and out of here would be clumsy, noisy, and slow—if I could do it. Considering the alternative, I could.

I took a deep breath and heaved up on stiff arms like a gymnast, feet swinging uselessly; then fell forward onto the deck with an appalling racket. I wriggled out and came up on my knees in time to see him leave the wheel and run forward. As he grabbed the shrouds and stumbled onto the side deck, the now unattended wheel turned and the boat swerved sharply to port. I was tossed against the starboard lifelines.

I grabbed a stanchion and stood up to meet his rush. The swing to port had moved the staysail boom to starboard; he hit it knee-high and pitched forward on his face as I dove over the starboard rail.

I hit the water, surfaced, bobbed frantically in the sixty-degree chop, fighting to get oriented. If I got confused, I could swim straight out to sea in the darkness. *Mixed Blessing* continued to port, turning a full circle. He was heading back. I spotted a flashing light and swam toward it, thinking like a robot: never mind the water never mind the cold never mind the boat arm over arm over arm over arm. The embankment was forty yards away.

I touched down, scrabbled up a slimy boulder, then another, another. When I paused to look back, I could see the boat sliding by to port. It began another circle. Using the great concrete cubes for cover, I scratched and scrambled toward the road at the top.

The boat made another pass and I crouched shivering in the lee of a boulder until it had glided by. I started climbing again, sneakers slipping on the greasy rocks. At the top, I dropped flat and looked outward. Without running lights to follow, the boat's course was hard to see in the near-dark. I stared for over a minute until I was sure it was heading due south, past the outer breakwater.

For a very private burial at sea, no doubt.

Reaction time.

I tottered through the little concrete park on the embankment, shuddering, making little dog noises in my throat. I kept recalling bluish dead legs, sailboat claustrophobia, furious bulk hurtling at me through the dusk, water like the electric chair, graceful menace of the circling boat. Feet, knees, hands scoured by the concrete sea wall, noisy sneakers leaking brine.

Step after step through the chill, too wretched to be furtive, I emerged into the ghastly orange blaze of sodium streetlights. No one about anyway. I scuttled past shuttered boat yards and yacht brokers up to the boulevard and over to my patient Rabbit, now alone in the public lot.

In out of the wind. Head on the steering wheel for ten seconds, twenty breaths. Then up the empty freeway, heater blasting, teeth clacking, pounding the wheel in frustration and grief.

Inexplicable grief: I never met the girl. Never saw a corpse before either. Young corpse; fragile; broken; flesh like cold plastic; razor stubble under my hand where I grabbed her calf. Toenails painted once; now peeling. Faint greasy sheen of sweat or oil. Sloping breast more obscene now than in that film.

Oh why?

My forebrain fuse blew mercifully and my driving center continued without the rest of me. Lanes were changed, signs noted, off-ramps negotiated. The Rabbit stopped on red, went on green, broke no laws, and deposited me at my door in Laurel Canyon. Clothes off, I crept into bed, and sank into sleep in sixty seconds.

8

THE MORNING AFTER WAS A LIQUORLESS HANGOVER COMplete with aches, shakes, and nausea. I was surprised to be alive and wishing I were dead. Outside, the bleak overcast that is L.A.'s only alternative to sunny blare. Inside, the ceiling fluorescents lit Sally's kitchen like a bus station. Sally sat very quietly across the table, still bundled in a sweatsuit after her three-mile morning run.

"Eat the eggs, Stoney."

"No."

"Then eat the toast at least. Come on now, drink the coffee too." I made a vague effort to obey. "Good boy."

Leaving me to it, Salley produced cheerful sound effects at the sink. The coffee nerved me for toast, the toast for eggs, and so I convalesced through breakfast.

"Any more coffee, Sally?"

"Sure." She put a hand on my shoulder as she poured. "More toast?"

"No thanks, but that was good."

She sat down again. "You sound better."

"Can you make sense out of all this?"

"I'm still turning it over. That poor girl."

I sipped my coffee, trying not to see the image of human debris tangled in the quarter berth. "I never met Lee Tolman, but something about her really got to me."

"I know."

"I liked her, even if she was a bit off center."

Sally started clearing breakfast. "Where does all this leave you?"

"Sherlock Holmes said something to me."

"One of your voices?"

"Mm. He said it makes perfect sense. We have only to learn how."

"Maybe, maybe not. You're sure it was Hammond?"

"Oh yes, he had the gate card and the combination to the hatch padlock. Besides, he was familiar with the boat. You can't just sail any strange boat, you know; it's not like driving a car."

"I'll take your word for it." She rinsed the plates.

"And I think he recognized me."

"You said it was almost dark."

"But I'd talked to him about Lee just a few hours earlier, and I stood on the dock for a while before going on board. He could have seen me through a window. I called out several times; perhaps he recognized my voice. And think of this: Lee was already down in the cabin, dead. If he hadn't recognized me, he would have come on deck, passed the time of day, and sent me on my way. No, Hammond knows I found Lee's body."

"But he doesn't know you're alive. When he last saw you, you were falling into twenty feet of ice water."

"It was only forty yards to shore."

"And almost dark. You said he circled several times before he gave up."

"True."

"So maybe he doesn't know whether you got out or not."

"Easy enough for him to find out."

Sally slapped the dish towel on the drain board and turned to me: "Then you'd better tell the police."

"Tell them what—that I broke into someone's boat? There was no one else on the dock to prove Hammond took the boat out. You can bet Lee's body's somewhere in the Pacific. And that boat's all fiberglass and plastic—very easy to clean up. By now, there's no evidence whatever."

"The girl is missing."

"She was missing two weeks ago. What does that prove about Hammond? No, I can't go to the police."

Sally looked thoughtful as she stowed plates on the top cupboard shelf, an easy reach from her five-foot, nine-inch height. Then she leaned against the counter, crossed her arms, and confronted me. "You don't *want* to go to the police."

"As a matter of fact, I don't."

"You're going to play Sherlock Holmes."

"I have an obligation."

"To what?"

Very hard to say the next thing. "I'm responsible for Lee's death. No, listen: yesterday I told Hammond I was looking for her. Hours later, he killed her. What else can I make of that?"

"You can't be sure. Besides, what can you do?"

"Get some help, to start."

"Such as?"

"You." Sally looked puzzled. "I've been thinking: you sold a computer to that big real estate company."

"Commercial Properties, Inc. In Century City."

"Are you friendly with the customer?"

"Too friendly. He kept trying to talk me into bed."

"Would he give you a rundown on Denise's studio? How much it's worth; what her chances are of selling it."

"That's what they bought the computer for. They can run an analysis on almost any commercial property in town. But what'll it tell you?"

"Denise is afraid she won't be able to sell her lot. That's the only hold the extortioners have on her. Her hope of selling's based on what Harry Hummel tells her—and he's not exactly Bernard Baruch."

"You want a professional judgment. Okay. Speaking of Denise, you'll have to tell her about Lee's death."

I nodded glumly.

Sally embraced me gently. "I guess you have to do this, Stoney. Please, please be careful."

She kissed me slowly and I took some comfort from the feel of her under her sweatsuit. But only some. She left to shower and dress.

I postponed the dreaded call to Denise by phoning Jerry the director.

"What's up, Winston?"

"Just checking in—you know. How'd the rest of the shoot go?"

"It didn't. Hammond never showed up after lunch."

"Oh? When did he leave?"

"I don't know; I was with you, remember? Nahan had six fits when he heard we had to pay the crew anyway. Cheap bastard."

"What did he say?"

"Nahan doesn't talk to us peasants. Just turned around and stalked out. But you shoulda seen his face. Hee hee, I loved it!"

"Okay, thanks."

"Uh, Winston?"

"Yeah?"

"What *are* you calling about?"

"As I said, just . . . checking in."

"You sound kinda weird. What are you snorting at 8:30 AM?"

"Well, thanks, Jerry. Take it easy."

If Hammond had gone straight to the yacht club, he'd have been there two hours ahead of me. Plenty of time.

My call to Denise raised only a cleaning woman who said Denise was at the studio. Hm, that's unusual.

Sally strode in, blasted shiny by a strenuous shower and disguised again as an executive. "I have a call in Century City. I'll see that real estate guy afterward."

"Thanks, Sally."

"Then I'm going to work out at the health club."

"You'll get muscle-bound."

"Not where it counts." Another gentle kiss, and then she was out the door.

Sunshine was replacing the overcast as I threaded the Rabbit through the morning rush, toward Tolman Studios. A massive figure was coalescing in the seat beside me: Doctor Samuel Johnson.

He trained his one good eye on Hollywood: "Those trees, Sir, are absurd."

"Which, the palm trees?"

He peered at the offending growths: scabrous trunks arcing fifty feet up to crowns of puny fronds. "Being too ill-made for either beauty or shade, they provide neither a pleasing prospect nor an umbrageous passage."

"They don't even produce fruit."

Doctor Johnson wiped his sizable nose absently on the sleeve of his rusty greatcoat. "Then what is the good of 'em?"

"I've never known."

"Harrumph." He blinked and squinted repeatedly in the growing glare. "I had an idea to see Africa once, but desisted from it. The tropics, Sir, are frivolous."

"Nothing wrong with that."

"In proportion, Sir, and I see no proportion here." He beat a tattoo on his knee with stumpy fingers.

"How's the dictionary coming?"

"Well enough, except for W, which is troublesome." Doctor Johnson heaved his bulk around to inspect me, knocking his great grey wig askew on the low Rabbit roof. "But you did not confine me to his less than capacious coach to inquire after my lexicography."

"I wanted some advice on a question of duty."

"When a man questions his duty, it is often because he is indisposed to do it."

"But what *is* my duty?"

The massive head cocked and the one good eye half-twinkled: "You do not believe in justice?"

"I wish I could."

The eye escalated to full twinkle. "And what did Mistress Sally say?"

"She guessed I had to do this. But that doesn't mean I agree with her."

"What a man is loath to say himself, he hopes to hear from others."

"You're fast with a proverb."

He half-bowed with clumsy good humor. "My stock in trade, Sir. Do not evade my point. You know, in fact, what you must do."

"The question is *how*?"

"Why, Sir: if you but study the play and the players in it, then cunning will bring you to them and wit prescribe questions for 'em; and if you reflect on their answers and observe their demeanor, then reason will unravel the plot and action procure a fit ending."

"Easy for *you* to say."

"In fact, Sir, such sentences are exhausting. Boswell did me no service in tidying my conversation for his book. The reputation that resulted has been an onerous burden."

"But in short, you agree with Holmes: discover the logic that solves the puzzle."

"I seldom speak 'in short,' but yes." Doctor Johnson fanned himself with a greatcoat lapel. "If I remain in your climate, Sir, I shall be cooked like a Sunday joint. May I return to my harmless drudgery?"

"Oh, of course; thoughtless of me."

The massive body was turning to smoke. "Not at all. I remain ever your most humble and obedient servant."

He was gone and suddenly the Rabbit felt positively roomy.

At the studio, Gladys Dempal said Denise was upstairs at the editing rooms. I passed along the looming corridor, up the stairs, and left toward the four little cells at the back of the building. The first door now proclaimed HARRY HUMMEL LIMITED.

Still an apt description of him. "Christ, Winston, aren't you ever home? I'm tired wasting quarters on your goddam machine."

I looked past him into the room. "Hello, Denise. I'm afraid we have to talk."

"All right."

"Could we go someplace?"

"Harry can hear."

"It's about Lee."

"He knows the whole story. I showed him the tape, remember?"

"I have very bad news, Denise: Lee is dead. She's been killed."

The shot turned into a freeze-frame: Hummel gaping behind the Moviola, Denise on the high editor's stool, me with my hand still on the door knob. Her face showed absolutely nothing.

Hummel sputtered to life: "Christ almighty! . . ."

"Hush, Harry." Denise still didn't move. "What . . . happened?"

"I found her on Isiah Hammond's boat. She was beaten to death."

"When?"

"Yesterday, around twilight."

"Why didn't you call?"

I told the whole story, ending with, "When I tried to call you at home this morning, the cleaning woman said you were here. I came right over."

She remained absolutely frozen while Hummel vaguely flapped his arms: "Jesus. I mean, who'd of? . . ."

"Please, Harry." She sat some more. "Are you sure it was Lee? You never did meet her."

I shook my head. "But I studied the tape very carefully. It was her body, all right." I stopped, surprised by a surge of angry grief.

Denise spun the shaft of the film synchronizer on the bench. Its ball bearings whickered faintly in the silence. She spun it again, deliberately, as if intrigued to learn how long it would revolve on a single twist.

Hummel shifted from foot to foot.

Denise sighed. "Dead." She pressed a catch idly and one of the synchronizer's multiple jaws sprung open. It gnashed mechanically when she pressed it down. "Dead. I can't take that in."

Hummel cleared his throat. "Thing is, this makes a couple problems with the studio."

Denise said gently, "Now now, Harry."

Hummel assumed a protective stance behind her, one hand on her shoulder, as if posing for a daguerreotype. "You gotta be practical. Like I said, we got a deal working. Arab types, right? They want things done real quiet."

I considered Hummel's unprecedented act of imagination. "Arabs."

Denise looked uncomfortably at the paw on her shoulder. "I guess Harry's right. We can't afford any public trouble until the studio's sold. Oh, I feel terrible saying that."

"You gotta be practical. Winston, you tell the cops?" I shook my head. "Great, then there's no problem."

"But I'll keep on looking."

Hummel shook his head. "No way. That's a wrap for you."

"What do *you* say, Denise?"

"I don't know. It's so awful about Lee. But she *is* dead. And you said there wouldn't be any evidence. I just don't know."

"What about the tape?"

"Well, I haven't heard any more and the sale is about to go through. I thought maybe just . . . let it alone. For now?" The last question was an appeal.

I wanted her to tell me explicitly. "So I'm not working for you anymore, is that it?"

Denise tried to smile. "Tell you what: I said you were on the payroll for two weeks. I'll pay you the twelve hundred dollars and you take the rest of the time off. Is that fair?"

Again, I felt resentful grief. Denise cared no more for Lee than Hummel did, or Hammond. So be it, then. I nodded.

She stood up uncertainly. "I'm going home now." Denise closed the door very slowly behind her, leaving me to Hummel.

"Hummel, why are *you* here?"

"Hey, what're friends for at a time like this?"

"But why do you have this cutting room?"

The usual shifty glance, then: "Well, she's got this empty room and I got like six spots to cut. We're sorta partners."

"And partners sorta get a cutting room rent-free."

"I mean I'm doing her a favor."

"What kind of favor?"

"Whadda you care? Just keep your nose outa my asshole."

"Hard to avoid."

"Huh?"

"Considering its percentage of your surface area."

I still had to connect with Low Profile's porn operation, so I needed an excuse to be here in the studio. "When do we start editing those commercials, Harry?"

Hummel's glance grew even shiftier. "You're not cutting the spots."

"Oh?"

"Thing is, I got this UCLA kid—in the film school? Says he wants the experience."

"And only fifty dollars for the job."

"Whaddya think I am? I'm paying a hundred."

I looked at him with ostentatious sorrow. "I don't know why I'm bothering with you, but I have to be honest."

Suspicious look: "Honest?"

"Think about it. Denise is paying me twelve hundred dollars and I've earned less than half of it."

"Yeah, she shoulda consulted me before she did that."

"So I really owe her a week's work."

A shrug: "That's her problem."

Shaking my head doubtfully as I continued miming my quandary: "But you said you and Denise were partners."

"Yeah, sorta."

"If you look at it that way, then I owe *you* the work."

I paused patiently until the dawn finally broke: "Hey, hell yes! You do."

"So you don't need to pay another editor."

Suspicion again: "Why you telling me this?"

I looked superior: "Standards, Harry."

Triumphant grin. "Damn right, and where do they get you?" He suddenly felt secure. "Okay, I got dailies coming out at noon—with the mag. I want 'em synced by tomorrow."

"The usual lab?"

"Yeah, and listen, go get a key from that old fart out front. I can't screw around here any more; I got things to do."

He bounced out. Nothing like saving a buck to put the bloom back in Hummel's cheeks.

And nothing like a cutting job to justify my presence on the lot. I pulled myself together as I descended the creaking stairway and headed for the front desk. Pausing at the lobby door to force a cheerful look by pure act of will, I swept into the lobby to court tubby Gladys with my most accomplished impression: W. C. Fields:

"Ah yass! There you are, my veal cutlet, casting your glow upon these dismal premises!"

Quick Gladys picked up Mae West: "Watcha *want*, big boy?"

"Merely to bask in your golden radiance, my dove, and perhaps a friendly hand of gin."

"I thought ya drank it from a *glass*." In her normal voice: "No wonder radio died. What's up, Stoney?"

"Turns out I was right, Gladys; Harry Hummel's setting up in cutting room one. Can I have a key?"

"Have to loan you the submaster again."

"I'll be here half the night syncing dailies. Can I get in and out?"

"That key'll do it."

"Thanks. See you later."

"Not if I see you first." Gladys must go back to Smith and Dale.

9

TRUDGING ACROSS THE HOT ASPHALT OF THE FILM LAB'S inner parking lot with my burden of priceless work print: 1,600 feet of 16mm Ektachrome film which in due course will celebrate Cutrate Cola in the form of six commercials, each precisely eighteen feet long. This would mean choosing the best 108 feet to use—or in the case of Hummel's footage, the worst 1,492 feet to dump.

I flung the film into the Rabbit's back seat next to the box of sound track and chugged through the motor-driven chain-link film lab gate. Then downtown on the Hollywood Freeway toward the office of our Great Metropolitan Daily and my friend Delbert Mund, whom I'd lured to a meeting with the promise of a drink.

I'd been thinking of Del when I told Sally I might enlist some friends to help me. He's the paper's third-string film critic, condemned to rating trash cranked out for drive-in movies on the cornpone circuit. He spends his days in dark communion with chain saw killers, berserk bikers, and psychic, sex-starved girls. Del is resigned to reviewing this drivel because he'd rather study bad films than no films at all. Considering Hummel's commercials, I'd guess Delbert is to reviewing what I am to directing. A sorry comment on us both.

Del was loitering in front of O'Leary's Cow, an instant Irish pub plugged into the lobby of a gunmetal skyscraper. Pushing through art nouveau doors, we walked a twisting wooden hallway whose changing levels had been built at great expense over the original concrete floor to a back room packed with grazing stockbrokers. We outraced three of them to a booth table defaced by factory-carved initials and obtained British pub mugs full of Budweiser.

"You look bleary, Delbert."

"You would too." Del pushed his horn-rims up and squeezed the bridge of his potato nose.

"What was it this time?"

"I swear I don't recall." He consulted notes on an envelope plucked from his vest pocket: "*Mincemeat*. Let's see, uh, driven bonkers by the sight of couples doing it on moonlit high school lawn, hero steals father's tractor and mows lawn, fornicators included. I stuck it out for forty minutes."

Del slumped in his seat, displaying an incipient dowager's hump. "Can you see a thirty-five-year-old man doing this for a living? Jee-zus!" He combed his remaining hair with his hand, one strand per finger. "Cheer me up, Stoney; tell me something nifty."

"Delbert, I have a possible scoop for you."

"I'll stick a press card in my hatband."

"Seriously; a potential story."

"Then find a reporter."

"A *media* story."

Del looked pained that I should have sunk so low: "Are you hustling PR now?"

"Not that kind of story. I'm talking financial hanky-panky."

"Oh, well that is exciting, but I was hoping for a Halloween feature."

"It isn't a joke, Del. Please."

Del's posture had degenerated until he resembled a pile of tweed suits put out to go to the cleaners. "I promise to remain conscious."

I told him what I'd learned about Isiah Hammond's finances: the disappearing love offerings, the troubles with the state, Hammond's less than ascetic life-style.

Del slouched even lower, if possible.

I outlined the week's events, ending with Lee Tolman dead in *Mixed Blessing*'s quarter berth. That sat him up an inch: "But how does she connect with the financial thing?"

"That's for you to find out."

He licked suds off his wispy mustache. "I have nothing to do with news; I barely *work* for the paper. What can I do?"

"Look Hammond up in the morgue—do they still call it that?"

"How would I know? I've never used it. Winston, they pay me to review garbage movies. I have no reason to go rooting in the files."

"Del, after all these years, *why* are you still reviewing garbage movies?"

"I'm missing your drift—if any."

"You're a perceptive, eloquent critic. Hell, your film reviews are better than the films."

Del's posture was approaching total collapse, but he seemed grudgingly pleased by my compliment. "It's a hopeless job. No one who's bright enough to read me ever sees the movies I write about. So what's the point?"

"Exactly. Isn't it time they gave you something worth your talents?"

"Oh my stars! And don't I just say those very words to the publisher every time we have lunch together." Del bestowed a look suitable for Hare Krishna panhandlers.

"I know, Del. But all the other critics write features too."

"They get the assignments."

"Why wait for an assignment? Remember that big studio scandal?"

"The embezzling mogul? Sure. The paper overlooked it for weeks after it broke. Embarrassing."

"All right, suppose the paper got onto Isiah Hammond *before* he hit the fan. And suppose you did it for them."

Del looked thoughtful. "They might even let me write it."

"Three thousand words: front page, left column."

"It's pretty feeble, Stoney. And I'm touched that you're waving my flag."

"Pure selfishness. Look, Hammond probably knows I found Lee's body, so I have to protect myself from him. But I haven't enough to tell the police and I've run out of leads. If you could give me some, then I could give *you* the story."

Del gazed at the bottom of his dimpled stein as if reading tea leaves in it. "I'll see what I can do. I have to go in today to write up *Mincemeat*." Del reassembled himself more or less upright. "You know, Stoney, you sound like a movie plot."

"So life *does* imitate art?"

"Don't force it. Life isn't a story line. If you force it into one, you'll get in trouble." Delbert looked uncomfortable, as if he'd been trapped into seriousness. "Quotations from Chairman Mund."

He blundered out, looking like a turtle in a three-piece suit.

Sitting on the redwood deck cantilevered out from the upper level of Sally's house, I watched my beloved landlady pursue her only known obsession: fitness.

"I meant it, Sally. You'll get muscle-bound."

"Thin too." Fingers laced together behind her head, she swept her elbows back and forth like a radar antenna.

"Why on earth do you want to be thinner?"

"I just don't want to be fatter, and we have spaghetti for supper."

"I'll cook; I can boil spaghetti. Did you find out about the studio?"

"Dynamite software. My customer accessed a regional data base and developed a whole spread-sheet analysis."

"I'm lost."

Squatting, hands on hips, Sally approximated a Cossack dance. "To be brief, Tolman Studios is not a hot property."

"I was afraid of that."

"It's too little. The stage isn't big enough for anything but commercials and—what do you call them?"

"Inserts?"

"That's it, so nobody'd want to use it as a studio."

"How about converting it to something else?"

She stood up, breathing hard, and the late afternoon sun turned her hide from tan to bronze. "Too tall. Nobody needs a one-story building forty feet high."

"They could tear it down and start over."

"Maybe. But my customer says those old soundstages were built like concrete bunkers. That's how they sound-proofed them, back in the early thirties."

"Expensive to raze them."

"That's what he says." She dropped to the deck and started puffing through a round of sit-ups.

"How about the land value?"

"Rising. That part of Hollywood's really (grunt) coming back. Studio's on two acres (grunt) and the zoning's right. That's enough virtue for one day."

"But the cost of pulling down the building would detract from the land value?"

"Affirmative." Sally sometimes lapses into executivese.

"Then it's unlikely that Denise will be able to sell the lot."

"I'd say so. If you'll make a salad too, I'll do the sauce. And sourdough bread with garlic butter. Yummy."

"We'll *both* need exercise."

"We can work something out."

"Garlic permitting. But first I have to go see Delbert Mund."

An hour later I was heading west through the warm twilight on Franklin Avenue toward Delbert's home in East Hollywood, spaghetti and garlic bread urging me to nap instead of work.

But Lee's body was out in the shipping lanes, a hundred fathoms down.

Weird orange sky as the sun behind me settled into the smog bank. Wonder what Del found in the newspaper morgue.

Regrettable word, that.

Del rents an old bungalow tucked in behind the ABC production center, a squat little clapboard house with ugly porch columns of cemented cobbles. Mozart floated in the warm air as I climbed four concrete steps, pushed the bell, and waited. The door swung open.

"Winston?" The voice seemed to come from a twelve-year-old boy and the reedy silhouette in the doorway confirmed this.

"Yes. I'm looking for Del."

"Come on in. We haven't met. I'm Janice."

Fully lit, the "boy" revealed bare feet with blood-red toenails, thin legs, and a spindly body in denim shorts and black leotard. Straight brown hair; large eyes behind larger glasses. Janice thrust out a hand to shake.

"Del and I are living together." This in the no-nonsense tone of a person who likes things defined. She led the way into the living room.

Del's home is a museum of movie trivia: posters, press kits, glossy stills in drugstore frames. A wall of shelved scripts and another half hidden by machines: videodisk, two videotape recorders, two monitors, and an elaborate audio system—plus thirty running feet of audio and video disks and cassettes. No wonder Del buys thrift shop suits.

He was lying on a sofa in his customary pile. "Nice timing, Winston; supper's on."

"I've eaten, thanks."

"You met Janice? What am I saying. Obviously, you met Janice. God, I'm turning to mush. Must be Alzheimer's disease. Sit down."

He pulled his necktie down to half-staff. "Big treat tonight: mock meatloaf and spinach salad. Never hook up with a vegetarian. The jug's full of chablis." Del discarded the record jacket he'd been reading. "Janice is a researcher at the paper so I turned her loose on your stuff."

Janice appeared on cue with two table settings and a glass for me. "Eat! I get really pissed off when people let good food get cold."

Del rolled minstrel show eyes toward heaven: "Mouf, don' fail me now!" Then he fell to obediently, chewed a bite of indeterminate protein, and shot me a look full of martyrdom.

Janice, on the other hand, dispatched her plate as if showing it who was boss. Then she gulped her wine and slumped back in her big armchair until all I could see was her small face floating above widespread, bony knees.

Her gold-framed eyes sparkled. "Well, Hammond has a file all right. You better take some notes."

"I'll remember."

She frowned at this unprofessional approach. "Okay, but it's complicated. I'll start with the bio. Hammond's fifty-one; came out of Arkansas; degree from a jerkwater Bible college; ordained by mail or something. No criminal record."

"Jan, do I have to eat the sprouts?"

"Don't interrupt, Del."

"Jeez, I feel like a cow."

"Anyway, he came out here; changed his name—he was born George Gutwillig—started a little church. Got pretty popular, but nothing special." Janice crunched a piece of ice like a dog biscuit. "Then he met one Nahan, comma, Wilton M."

"I know him."

"Nahan's some kind of financial genius. He talked the congregation into buying a little radio station, put Hammond on the air, and started an empire."

"With the contributions sent in."

"Well, the elders—or whatever they call them—complained. Said the church wasn't seeing any money. They tried to get control back, but Nahan set up a foundation independent of the church. He got Hammond to quit the church and keep the radio station, plus real estate and other operations."

"Such as?"

"Oh, a travel agency."

"A what?"

"Sure: set up to send the faithful on Holy Land tours and worldwide missions, ho ho. And all tax-exempt. Of course they did a *tiny* bit of commercial business too—like about ninety percent. Needless to say, the government got intrigued and finally sued them."

"What happened?"

"It's been in the courts for years now. You see, Nahan set up front corporations in five states and bank accounts from here to Bermuda. So every time someone goes to a court, Nahan shifts the assets out of its jurisdiction."

Janice scratched a knobby knee. "By now they're really flying, with a Bible college and a TV station. That station is a gold mine. They have a satellite hook-up—broadcast all over the country."

"And Hammond rakes in the money."

"That's the cute part: his salary is exactly one dollar a year. Of course, he has an unlimited expense account which is never audited, a Rolls Royce to ride around in, and a 'parish house' near Beverly Hills, though there isn't any parish."

"What do his faithful think of all this?"

"What else? A conspiracy by the secular humanist media to smear a man of God."

"A very smart operator."

"Wrong!" Janice poured four inches of chablis into her glass. "Hammond's just the front man but Nahan's the brains. At least some of the holding corporations and dummy foundations are in Nahan's name. He controls the money."

"I saw him and Hammond fighting over money."

"Nahan's got a long history: fancy real estate scams, funny bonds—you name it."

"Cold-blooded sod."

"But things are heating up now. The attorneys general of three states are talking to each other. The FCC is on Hammond's case about the station license, and the IRS is in hot pursuit."

"Did Del tell you about Lee Tolman?"

"That was awful."

"Why would Hammond want to kill her?"

Primly: "I'm a researcher, not a psychic." She joined Del on the sofa, draping a fragile arm over his thick shoulders.

"Please, Janice, help me put this together."

Reluctantly: "I'll go this far: her death is probably not connected to the money business. Even if she really did work as Hammond's secretary, she'd never seen any financial stuff. That all goes through Nahan's office."

I recalled the iron-gray Matron at her word processor. "But why else would he kill her?"

Del stared at the movie posters taped to the ceiling. "Accident? Crime of passion? Who can tell? You know, Stoney, you're hunting connections which probably don't exist. I told you: only movies have plots."

"I don't think so. I discussed it with a couple of, um, friends and they agree. They said the trick is to uncover the logic that drives this business. Then all the connections will be obvious."

Del shook his head stubbornly. "I'm not against cause and effect. But in life, things don't hook up in long chains like polymers."

"Maybe. Well, thanks for all your work, Janice. What do you think, Del? Is there a story there?"

"A dandy! And the paper printed it months ago. Where do you think Jan got all that stuff? No chance for me, though."

"Sorry."

"Never mind; I'm intrigued. Maybe I'll tune in tonight and watch Hammond sing his song."

"No way!" Janice stretched like a scrawny cat. "I want to go to bed."

"Well okay, I'll put the timer on and tape it."

I thanked them again and left.

10

CHUGGING THROUGH THE HOT, DRY NIGHT—OPEN WIN-
dows no substitute for the Rabbit's busted air conditioner—
toward Tolman Studios. Maybe I should sync those dailies
now; it would give me a chance to think. What Janice said
makes Nahan as important as Hammond—to the church
anyway. Have to check him out.

Nice about Del and Janice: a reminder that there's
someone, somewhere, for everybody.

The studio lot was deserted except for a dusty van
parked near the lobby entrance. I parked the Rabbit and
started for the front door, juggling film, sound track, and
keys. Doors opened on both sides of the van.

Paranoia time. Remembering Hammond's unhealthy
interest in me, I swung into a quick U-turn, regained the
Rabbit, and drove back out of the lot.

Sure enough, the van followed. Unbelievable: I've
lived so close to movies, I was finally in one—somehow
absorbed into a cheap action picture, playing out clichés. A
car chase, for God's sake; this couldn't really happen.

Could it? Test the thesis: left on Santa Monica; the van
copied. Right on Vine; the van followed. North all the way
up to Franklin with the van maintaining its distance. Left
on Franklin; the van turned left as well.

And so on, through four miles and six turns, to Laurel
Canyon Boulevard, the van precisely half a block behind.
Up into the canyon proper, corkscrewing around crazy little
streets canted at ruinous angles, past eccentric box houses
on stilts, along scrub-coated hillsides full of snakes, coyotes,
and other vermin. Inky labyrinth outside the Rabbit's head-

lights, except for two bright spots trailing behind. Another mile and I'd be home.

Home? I didn't want to take them home. I swerved suddenly into an uphill lane, driving as fast as darkness and potholes allowed. Then faster, pushing it dangerously on the curves, twisting around Toyotas and Jeeps and Porsches parked half off the asphalt. Skidding; recovering; wishing I'd seen to that bad steering linkage.

The van dropped back a bit; it didn't handle like the Rabbit. But my old engine was half shot. Give them a long straightaway and they'd catch me. I prayed for curves; prayed I'd stay on the road when I hit them.

A cross street. I swung right without stopping, then down fifty yards and yanked the wheel hard left into another lane. Did I lose them? No: headlights behind.

The Rabbit picked up speed on a downhill straight, then screeched into a dead-end circle. Stuck! I slewed around the circle, then snuggled up against the hillside by the exit. I killed the lights.

A surge of crazy joy, despite the situation, like ol' Burt Reynolds truckin' 'shine in his TransAm. Joy faded fast as the van roared past into the dead-end turning circle. I gunned the Rabbit and shot downhill again, hitting the lights just in time to see a 180-degree turn. The van's lights were visible as I screamed around the bend and back to the cross street; then right again, always uphill. If I could reach Mulholland Drive at the top, I could lose them.

I wound upward past the last houses, past the streetlights, up the dark, empty road now bordered only by trees and scrub. Couple of miles now; just a couple.

No chance: there was that deadly uphill straightaway. The van gained steadily, then shot past. Fifty yards up, it braked and spun sideways to block the road. No room to turn; no time to back down.

Two figures jumped out of the van as I stopped ten feet away. One crouched in my headlights holding something in classic, two-handed firing position. I hit the door lock on my side and was reaching for the other button when the second figure yanked the door open. A dull, bulky weapon pointed at my eye. He reached across and pulled my door handle. The first man opened my door and hauled me out into the hot night.

They were just shapes in the dark: a fat man and a tall man. Fat man said, "Put him back in his car. No, you asshole, the passenger side. *I'll* drive. You turn the truck around."

The tall man walked back toward the van. In the Rabbit's headlights, he revealed a beaky nose, red nylon warm-up jacket, and running shoes.

The fat man squeezed into the driver's seat—a bearded troll in a lumberjack shirt with a stubby pistol in his thick hand. He looked at me without expression, wheezing from his exercise.

The tall man pointed the van in its original direction and started uphill. The Rabbit followed, lurching as the fat man tried to shift, steer, and keep me covered. We wound up the deserted road through several switchbacks while I tried to ignore my dry mouth. There was no conversation.

Two hairpin reverses higher, the van pulled off and stopped at a scenic viewpoint. The fat man parked the Rabbit facing the drop-off, about three feet back from the edge, then wheezed, "Out!" He covered me as he too left the car.

In front of us, the hillside plunged at a sixty degree angle toward a bright blue kidney target: someone's lit swimming pool eight hundred feet below. On the other side of the road behind us, the same slope rose up toward the next switchback above.

The tall man trotted up and the fat man yelled at him, "Go get the truck. Pull it up behind here so we can push him off."

"How do we keep him from locking his brakes?"

"Smash him on the forehead first. It'll look like he hit the windshield."

The tall man returned to the van and started the engine. As he revved it, the gears crunched and the wheels started spinning. The fat man looked exasperated.

I edged around until my back was to the Rabbit.

The fat man swung to cover me: "Hold it!" I stopped and he ended up facing me, his back to the van.

The motor roared again and the spinning wheels threw gravel up onto the roadway. The fat man glanced angrily back at the truck. Then a mighty bellow as the truck started inching backward.

The fat man lost all patience: "Jesus Christ!" He swung his bulk to look.

I punched into his soft gut as hard as I could. He *oofed*! noisily, turning toward me. I backhanded him in the face with the heel of the same fist. His nose made a sound like snapping chicken bones. The fat man screamed and grabbed at his face.

Fat man inspected his bloody hands as I looked around. The drop in front was suicide. Across the road and up the opposite slope. At least they couldn't follow me in the truck.

I scrabbled through the dry scrub in total blackness—swarming up, sliding back, grabbing anything, small bushes yanking loose in my hands, rain of dirt and stones marking my trail up over boulders, brush, and sod. Shouts from below as they followed. Making a dangerous racket myself, I crashed through the tinder. No pausing, no looking down.

I was brought up short by a six-foot granite escarpment. Had to go sideways. I crept along the rock wall to the right, sneakers slipping, cascades of pebbles giving me away. Thrashing and crashing continued down below me. I spotted a small hollow beside a boulder. Maybe I could roll it down on them. Trial heave. No, it must weigh a thousand pounds. I paused to listen, opening my mouth, nose, and throat to keep my breath from whistling. The crashing sounds were fifty yards to my left now, and twenty below.

The tall man shouted: "I lost him."

"Hey!" from the fat man back on the road below. "Get back here. There's a better way."

Scrambling sounds diminished as the tall man retreated.

Looking around the boulder, I could see the outline of the van. The tall man opened the rear doors, disappeared inside, reemerged with a burden, and returned to the fat man. Brief instructions too low to hear, then the tall man started carrying the object along the base of my scrub hillside, pouring from it as he went.

The fat man lit a match.

You have to see a California brushfire to understand its terror. The scrub is so dry it actually explodes, shooting flames twenty feet high. The fire burns in long lines, snaking over the ground contours, advancing in sudden rushes, reversing itself, leapfrogging a hundred feet to ignite a new spot just beside you. Hot dusty winds sweep up canyon walls, driving the flames in sheets. Eucalyptus trees blaze like leafy beacons. The sound is as frightful as the heat and flames—a crackling riot over an almost subsonic roar.

This fire was no exception. Fifty feet long at the base of my slope, it rushed up toward me at thirty feet a jump, boiling with acrid smoke and sounding like a giant stomping a million Tinkertoys. Plenty loud to cover *my* noise, so I scrambled farther to the right, sweating and cursing the dirt in my eyes.

I'd moved another fifteen yards sideways when the fat man shouted, "Okay, up to the top."

"What if he comes down?"

"I'll watch down here."

The tall man jumped in the van and headed up the road. The next switchback would bring him to a spot just above the fire. They were hoping the flames would drive me out of cover onto the road above. Instead, I scrabbled down and sideways, trying to check the fire's direction. But there was only a confusion of black night, white murk, and searing yellow-red.

It seemed to burn straight up the hill. I reached the road below and looked up it toward the Rabbit and the fat man beside it, gun in hand. Suddenly, his head turned toward the far edge of the fire and he lumbered away in that direction. I scuttled across the road and keeping low, ran through the poisonous air to my car. I crouched in the shelter of the driver's door and looked upward. An immense cloud of smoke rolled uphill. Jumping in, I switched on the ignition, slammed the door, screeched backward away from the drop-off, and swung the Rabbit's nose downhill. A fat form in my rearview mirror was silhouetted in the flames. It wheeled around.

I heard nothing above the fire's thunder, but a sunburst of crazed glass erupted across my rear window. I shoved the car viciously into first gear and screamed away in a splash of white gravel.

A mile down the mountain road, a pair of fire engines roared past me, headed uphill. L.A. firemen are unbelievably responsive—especially to brush fires above residential areas. They would drive Fat and Tall away in the opposite direction and save me from roasting to a pile of charred bones and melted fillings.

Shouldn't have thought of that. Suddenly I had to pull over. I stumbled out of the car and onto the shoulder. Then I threw up. Shaking and sweating, I crawled back into the driver's seat. I managed to turn the ignition key and the starter shrieked in protest: the engine was already running. I put the car in gear and wobbled down the long hill home.

The shaking and nausea were waning now, leaving me scratched and dirty and tired beyond imagining. Once again, I drove home on automatic pilot.

Curled up on my bed, exhausted, smelling sweat and smoke, listening to my twitchy breathing, bedspread embossing my cheek. Paralyzed.

My front door opened and shut. If it was my playmates again, I didn't care.

"Stoney? You back? I saw the Rabbit." Sally's voice coming slowly on-mike. "I left a demonstrator in my trunk. Can you come help me lift—my God!"

Her hands on me, turning me on my back. "What's the matter? You're filthy. Are you all right?"

I just stared.

"Stoney, what happened to you?"

"Some of Hammond's meatballs found me."

"When?"

"What is it, ten o'clock? An hour ago."

"Are you hurt?"

"No."

"You're shaking."

"Damn right."

"Oh Stoney! I warned you this morning. How stupid can you get? Come on."

"What?"

"You can't just lie there. Up!"

Powerful hands under my arms hauled me up off the bed and propelled me, shambling, into the bathroom.

"Look at you: shirt torn, covered with filth, cuts, scratches. Don't do that; stand up! Come on, Stoney, *stand up*!"

Belt jerked open, pants yanked down, shirt peeled off. I sank onto the toilet while Sally discarded my shoes and socks and wrestled off my pants and shorts. Shivering, naked, as she turned on the water. Then I was heaved up again and shoved into my big stall shower.

"Clean yourself."

Standing there an inch below the shower head, feeling the hot sting on my new little bald patch. Sally was talking loudly over the shower noise: "Who was it?"

"I said."

"Hammond's people?"

"Who else?"

"Are you washing? Wash, Stoney."

Weaving in the stream. "Okay."

"I'll get your robe." The bathroom door closed, leaving me in the roar of hot water.

Five minutes later, Sally found me still swaying there, a sopping zombie.

"Oh Stoney!" She stripped and crowded in with me. "Give me the soap. Washcloth. Come on, Baby: the square blue fuzzy thing. *That's* a boy."

She washed me like a nurse processing a patient: face, neck, arms, chest. "Turn!" She rubbed the foaming cloth around my back, between my shoulder blades. It was beginning to feel good.

"Now rinse." I revolved obediently under the nozzle, coming slowly back to life.

Sally soaped the cloth again, squatted, and washed my feet and legs, scraping at the grot above my heels. Looking down, I saw her yellow hair darkening in splotches as the spray caught it, and a line of spine bumps dwindling down her back. Her shoulder blades shifted as she scrubbed.

"Rinse again." I did, starting to enjoy the stinging stream.

Standing up, Sally discarded the washcloth and revolved the soap in sudsy hands. "As long as I'm in here . . ." She plastered her neck, arms, and shoulders with foam. "I'm a little rank myself."

Glancing downward as she turned, Sally noticed my growing interest. She smiled. "Why Stoney! Does that mean you've come back to life? Come here."

She wrapped me in a soapy embrace. "Sally. Um, Sally . . ."

She smiled and nodded gently, then leaned back against the blue tile wall. Her arms circled my neck.

We stood locked together in the hot spray, enfolded, unmoving except to tense, relax, and tense again. I could have stayed suspended there forever.

As Sally pushed her hips against me, she drew her head back and the water suddenly coursed down her face, blinding her. She laughed and spluttered, then whispered, "Stoney, let's get dry now."

We toweled each other with slow playfulness, then ambled toward my rumpled bed to finish.

"You know, Stoney, you're even better when you're tired."

"Hm?"

"Slow and easy. Very sexy."

"Not hard to manage; I could barely move."

"It's not how *much* you move." Sally chuckled. "My husband was the strenuous type."

"Standing up in a hammock, and so forth?"

"Oh, nothing like that; that takes imagination." She burrowed under my outflung arm. "No, he just thought he had to be a pile driver. Slap, slap, slap."

"I get the picture."

Long sleepy pause, then: "Stoney?"

"Mm."

"Give this up."

Silence.

"Well why won't you?"

Another long pause while I figured it out myself. Then, "I was frightened tonight; terrified. That hasn't happened to me since—well I don't even know when. I didn't like the feeling."

"Understandable."

"I despised myself for being frightened and I hated the men who did it to me."

"So now you're going to get back at them."

"No, but I'm keeping after this business."

A sigh; then, "What'll you do next?"

"Tomorrow I'll sync Hummel's dailies. That's a great aid to contemplation. And as soon as I think of something . . ." I shrugged, shifting my arm.

"Stoney?"

"Mm?"

"I'm glad you just took a shower."

"Me too."

"Because you just put your armpit over my face."

"Sorry." I shifted back.

"Well don't go *away*."

"Never."

Sleepily: "I like the sound of that."

"Then there's comfort yet."

11

I HID MYSELF IN THE SPOOKY GLOOM OF DENISE'S EMPTY studio, locked tight on this hot Saturday morning.

There's no retreat like a cutting room, a monastic cell crammed with venerable objects: benches and bins, reels and rewinds, sound readers and synchronizers. For an altar, the metallic green Moviola, bristling with arms and pulleys, its improbable contours witness to half a century of piece-meal evolution. Modern machines may work faster, but the Moviola is like a concert grand: at once a technological wonder and a demanding, personal instrument. An editor *performs* on a Moviola.

Editing routines are soothing rituals like saying the rosary: snipping long reels of dailies into separate shots; winding each into a tight roll, picture with sound; taping and labeling; shelving in neat boxes or tidy upright rows.

An editor presumes to dismantle life, assign the pieces meaning, then reassemble a more coherent reality. As pure an act of faith as any.

And just as pointless, when the reordered reality started out as Hummel's cola footage. I ran the shots back and forth, braking at the cut point, grease-penciling the frame, splicing the shots with Mylar tape: clear for picture, white for sound.

Like driving, cutting frees part of the brain to spin along alone. Hammond knew I'd got out of the water alive —last night proved it. And now the world was not safe for Winston.

I squinted at a misplaced trim too short to put in the Moviola. Drat Hammond for shooting 16mm film. Can't see the bloody image without a loupe.

Assume Lee's film was made here, whether by Mr. Low Profile or Pepe or whoever. Assume the original footage is here in the studio. I searched their cutting room and found nothing, but editors like to keep their stuff handy; it's a habit. And they like to keep it safe in a vault.

Or the next best thing: a film storeroom. Like the one just down the hall.

Poking a cautious head into the dark corridor, I listened to the silence. Then I took out my submaster key, left my own door unlocked in case of rapid retreat, scuttled down the hall, unlocked the storeroom, slipped inside, shut the door, hit the light.

The harsh fluorescent washed ranks of silver cans shelved vertically like books, titles lettered on taped rims. Work prints, out-takes, dirty dupes—stuff not worth vaulting. Stored temporarily, years ago, then forgotten. Some cans were dated: 1939, 1942. That meant the film was nitrate stock. Glad I didn't write Denise's fire insurance. Unpromising: there must be close to five hundred cans here; take a week to open every one.

At the far end against the wall, six cans stuck out an extra inch. Or maybe they were *pushed* out by something behind them. Sure enough: a four hundred foot, 16mm can. Unmarked. Trophy in hand, I buttoned up the storeroom and retired to my sanctum.

The can contained a work print on a plastic core, tail end out. I rewound it onto a reel, then fed the head end into the Moviola.

And there it was: the room, the bed, the stud, the redhead girl. I had the original film—or at least a work print struck from it. I stared blankly at the little glass screen as footage snickered through the machine into the bin on the far side. I stopped the picture on a close-up—the face in those high school pictures: the same remote smile, same puzzled green eyes under a cloud of carrot hair. I released the hand brake, allowing movement to resume in this tiny world.

The dance continued through the usual positions until at length, the stud mimed ecstasy and pulled free. What a contemptuous gesture: the ritual besmirching of the submissive female. But Lee's big eyes stayed calm and her smile remained, as if she were really someplace else.

I wearily rewound the film out of the canvas bin, careful of the fragile splices. Something nagged me, something wrong about that film. I nerved myself to look at it again: same dreary ritual, same insulting ending, same tranquil face.

The face.

A quick rewind, then I ran the film again, this time on the bench-top viewer where I could pull it through at high speed, hunting Lee's face. There . . . and there . . . and there . . . always a tight close-up. I checked all the medium and full shots. Confirmed: her face did not appear recognizably in any of them. Lee's close-ups were shot separately and cut into the film, almost as if the head and body belonged to two different people.

Wishful thinking: close-ups are *always* shot separately. Still, I double-checked it. The edge numbers coding the medium and long shots belonged to the same roll of film, while Lee's close-ups had totally different numbers. Yes, but if they'd shot two-camera style, there *would* be different rolls. Not conclusive.

I went through it forward and backward, shot-by-shot—fast, slow, single frame. Nothing. Again. Nothing. By now the content was quite meaningless. I wanted to believe it but I couldn't prove it.

The work print was now dirty from looping onto the floor. Rewinding, I pulled it through my cotton-gloved fingers to clean it. Some of the splicing tapes were working loose.

Tapes.

Stopping the reels, I put the film back into the viewer at random: long shot; medium shot; Lee's close-up; another medium shot. I pulled the film and checked the splices.

And there was the proof: Lee's close-ups were spliced into the film with the narrow straight-edged tapes produced by a guillotine splicer. But all the other shots were joined with the wider, ragged-edged tapes cut by a *Rivas*-type splicer. An editor may use both splicers, but not at the same time. Lee's close-ups were replacements, added later to the original film. The girl who lay writhing on grimy sheets was not Lee Tolman.

But she *was* the girl I left on the boat, broken beyond mending.

It sank in slowly: Lee Tolman was not dead. *Not. Dead.* I felt like giggling or yelling or buying cigars. My cheeks cramped from grinning.

Not dead.

And yet, the logical structure that was building had been destroyed like a cube puzzle twisted once too often. Another girl had been killed—another redhead connected with Hammond and Lee. Connected somehow. *How?* Give the cube another turn.

Lee didn't make the film, but she had consented to those close-ups, apparently naked on matching bedsheets. One doesn't find such shots in home movie outtakes. No, her close-ups were made specifically for insertion in that film, and she must have known it.

Made by another somebody who lit the set, shot the footage, had it processed, cut it in. Somebody who had access to the original dirty movie.

Somebody like the proprietors of *Night Nurse Nooky*. Test this new pattern.

I made a one-minute reconnaissance mission to the adjacent cutting room. *Night Nurse Nooky* was now neatly canned and labeled, trims boxed. But the equipment was still ready for use and the editor's personal junk was all over the cutting bench, which displayed a note grease-penciled onto a tablet: "Phil: Finished Nooky. Call me when you get dailies from Saturday's shooting. Mel."

Today, of course, was Saturday.

*   *   *

I crept along the bleak hallway and down the stairs, feeling like a fugitive in an old Warner Brothers gangster film. Wrong approach; I should look as if I belonged down here. Straightening up, I loafed up to the big soundstage door and pulled the handle. Locked. No red light on, no way to hear through the soundproofed wall. Stymied.

A quick passage to the lobby. Half a dozen parked cars were visible through the window, so somebody was here. Thinking: soundstage loading doors no good; they're worked from inside. Try the roof. The air-conditioning's up there. Must be access somehow.

I snuck around to the outside staircase at the back of the building. Up the fragile iron steps, treading near the wall, cursing Denise for not maintaining her studio. As I dusted railing rust from my hands, I saw a shed-like structure at the center of a web of metal ducts. The padlock was broken; blessing Denise for not maintaining her studio.

It took a moment before I made out the trap door beneath the dust. I pulled the ring handle gently: nothing. Harder. Surprisingly, the door swung upward without much sound. Another minute to adjust to the even dimmer light beyond, then I recognized the slat floor of the grid that spanned the soundstage, eight feet below the roof. I eased down the filthy old ladder and paused inside.

The stage floor lay thirty feet below me, with the hospital set lit and working. Framed by the lighting catwalks floating above it, the distant scene resembled a TV picture. The usual couple on the bed, the woman astride, partner largely invisible beneath.

Wisps of talk drifted up unemphatically: "Great. Keep going. Camera two, get a reverse."

A hairy figure took his hand-held Eclair to the head of the bed, just outside the other camera's frame.

"Okay, now doggie-style. Fine, Honey, fine. Camera two, get the close-up."

Hairy carried his camera to bedside: "I only got maybe fifty feet left."

"Then don't shoot until he comes. Let us know, Chuck."

"Pretty soon." Chuck the stud sounded abstracted as he tried to predict his timing. "Get ready."

"Set, camera two?"

"Any time, C.B." Hairy was quite the wit.

"Talk to us, Chuck."

"Here I come."

"Rolling, two?"

"Rolling."

"Now," laconically from Chuck.

"I'm out." From Hairy.

"No sweat; we got it. Now collapse, both of you; go ahead and collapse." The tiny couple sprawled. "Fine, kids." To Hairy: "You reload yet?"

"Coming." Hairy grabbed a fresh film magazine, deftly pulled the exposed strip of film into an arch to check it, and slapped the magazine on the Eclair body. "All set."

"Right. Camera one, cut. Camera two, get her reaction." Hairy moved in on the woman's face. "Big smile, honey; that's good."

She mimicked his grimace.

"And cut, camera two. Great. Okay, relax."

Chuck swung around to sit on the edge of the bed. "Who's got a cigarette?"

Honey left the frame and the director walked in:

"Okay, redress for the other room, Lena." A scrawny blond woman appeared with a framed picture and started changing the set dressing. The director looked off the set, shading his eyes. "Hey Pepe?"

And Pepe Delgado strode forward importantly, dressed in his usual velour shirt and sharp footgear.

The director consulted a clipboard. "Henry and Dolores are up next. Jesus: Chuck again? Pretty rough on him. And Peeper; where's Peeper?"

From overhead, Pepe's parody Latin gestures looked even less believable: "I told her ten o'clock today, but you know that one: she runs on Mexican time."

"We can't hold up the shoot."

"You can use the black one. Put Peeper in when she shows up. Can't you handle this thing? I have important matters at hand."

The director's face was unreadable down there. "Yeah."

"All right, my friend, I will come back later." Wheeling about, Pepe made his exit.

The director stared after him, then: "Lena? How long till the set's ready?"

"Gimme ten?"

"Go ahead. If Chuck has to work again, he'll need the time." With a disgusted shrug, the director left my frame.

I retraced my route up out of the stage, through the air-conditioning shed, across the roof, and down the rusty ladder. Rounding the building, I saw Pepe drive out of the front lot, so I knew the story I was developing would play. This time, I marched up to the soundstage door and pushed the buzzer smartly. No response. I leaned on it. Finally, the big door cracked and the scrawny blond peered out.

"What?"

I summoned a harmless smile. "Pepe said Peeper was coming in at ten today."

"She's late."

"He said she might be, so I should just hang around and wait."

Suspicious look, so I added a stitch to my embroidery: "Still shooting *Night Nurse Nooky*?"

"We wrapped it two days ago. It only took a morning."

"Oh, right. Well, Pepe said to wait on the stage. Said I shouldn't be out where people can see me."

Her minute nod affirmed the logic of this. "Okay." She let go of the door handle and returned to dressing the set. I slipped inside and closed the door.

I played "Pepe Said" on the director too when he looked my way: "Hi! Pepe said to wait in here for Peeper."

His beard shifted as he pursed invisible lips. "She

comes and goes." Then, smiling at his brilliant joke, "that's her job." I mimed appreciation. "But I'll tell you something: never mix talent and management."

"How do you mean?"

"She thinks because she's Pepe's old lady, she can do what she pleases."

"I see your point. Pepe doesn't spend much time on the set."

"He likes to play the big producer."

"I know. Well, I'll just stay out of your way while I wait for Peeper."

He nodded indifferently and wandered off. I settled into a canvas chair, assuming the bored, patient look of someone who belonged there.

By rearranging pictures and furniture, the scrawny blond had created a different hospital room—not that the neanderthals who watch this trash would notice. In fact, the layout was too similar to need relighting, so they were ready to go again.

Chuck was limping around in a phony leg cast and hospital shortie nightgown. A slender black man accompanied him, looking distinguished in lab coat with prop stethoscope. Honey's vast toffee breasts strained the seams of her nurse's dress.

The other actress was a striking South American type with dark hair and imperial eyes. The director checked her over: "Fix your dress, Dolores." She pulled her white uniform together and buttoned it with slender fingers.

"Okay, Chuck: on the bed. Hook your leg up."

"Do I have to screw in this trapeze?"

"That's the gimmick: you get laid in traction."

"Jesus!" But Chuck climbed obediently aboard.

"Here it is, guys: you nurses come in and start giving Chuck a bath. Honey, you egg him on—you know."

Honey grinned.

"Dolores, you see he's getting interested, so you tip Honey the wink and you both go after him."

"So Doc, they're really going at it when you come in. You get the picture and join the fun. That's about it."

The "doctor" nodded soberly. "Who takes on who?"

"Checkerboard: all black and white."

Honey grinned at the doctor: "Sorry, Baby." He smiled back.

They continued to choreograph the orgy with the professional detachment of decorators arranging furniture. Camera one was set to cover the basic angles while Hairy prepared for cutaways with hand-held camera two. By now the cast was a tangle on the bed.

"Okay, let's make one."

Chuck poured some baby oil from a bottle provided by the scrawny blond.

"Go ahead and roll. Mark it, Lena." She thrust a slate labeled *Hospital Orgy* before camera one, clapstick open to show this was M. O. S. (without sound).

"Sticks out; action." And the scenario, such as it was, unfolded. Dolores and Honey were quite professional about keeping open to the camera as they attacked the patient Chuck. Hairy moved around grabbing close-ups, accompanied by an assistant holding a small lamp with which to banish gloom from shaded private parts. Like a ringside announcer, the director called descriptions blow-by-blow.

The effect was anything but erotic because, as always, the event was overwhelmed by the process of filming it. For all the randy slap and tickle, they might just as well have been recording an assembly line procedure.

It's sad, but in a sense, they were.

At length, the director stopped the take. "What's wrong, Chuck?"

"What do you think, after ten minutes?"

"Just relax. Fluff him a little, girls."

Honey appraised the situation with a professional eye, then swung off the bed. "Don't hold your breath, folks." She started in my direction. As she oscillated toward me, I tried to compute the forces generated by her mighty breasts. For Honey, walking must be like fighting a pair of gyroscopes.

She plonked down in the chair beside mine. "Well, what you think so far?"

"What can I say?"

"You git off watchin' people?"

"No, I'm more a doer. Just waiting for Peeper Martin."

"Then you *must* be a doer. But she ain't here."

"I know."

"An' I'll lay you odds she don't show till after lunch. I *know* that girl." She scratched a tan thigh.

"Lee Tolman ever hang out around here?"

"Oh yeah; couple times. Like, she don't work with us; you know? But she comes in."

"Recently?"

"Uh-huh. Hey Lena! Gimme that J. an' J." Scrawny passed her the baby oil. Rising, Honey shrugged off the open uniform and sat down again, negligently bare.

"Funny thing: I don't sweat hardly, even in the lights." Shaking a puddle of oil into a palm, she started massaging her thigh. "But sex suppose to make you sweat, you dig? So I got to fake it." She coated her left thigh, then started on the right. "I mean, can't have a sexy gal don't sweat, you know?"

It seemed about time to acknowledge this performance: "An' Miz Scarlett, you *know* you cain' show yo' bosom 'fo' four aclock."

Long pause while she trained bland eyes on me, then Honey smiled with a lovely sweetness, and when she replied, the chitlins had vanished from her speech. "Anyway, it helps my skin. What do you want with Lee?"

By now, my cover story had a lapidary shine: "Lee's got some money coming from her stepmother. The mother paid me to look for Lee, so she could get the money. I've never met Lee, but everyone I've talked to seems to think she's an unusual person."

Another bland stare, then Honey handed me the bottle. "Do my back, will you?" She leaned forward in the chair. I spattered oil between her shoulder blades, then rubbed her skin as clinically as possible. She remained silent, her face invisible.

"There you go."

She sat up. "Thanks; give me the bottle." She dappled herself with oil while I kept my eyes on her face and wondered where to wipe my hands.

Her smile grew mildly taunting. "Keep talking."

"That's all, really."

"Hm." She spread the oil, watching my face with that bland look. "Am I bothering you?"

"A bit, yes."

"Why?"

This was becoming tiresome. "Partly because you're shining me on, and I didn't do anything to justify that."

"Jus-tee-*fy* that!" The chitlin' dialect returned for one phrase, then she resumed her normal speech. "What's the other partly?"

"I'm tempted to like it."

"What's wrong with that?"

"Nothing, if it's part of liking all of you. But I don't even know you—except that you do a nice impression of Hattie McDaniel."

She began oiling her arms, but absently, as if she were taking a solo sunbath. "What are you really doing here?"

I looked at her. No longer teasing, she lounged as unself-consciously as if her shiny flesh were shrouded in a tent. Like her hands, her face was oddly slender, with grave, knowing eyes. She regarded me patiently, like a schoolteacher waiting for an answer from a slow child.

Something about her encouraged candor. "There's another film—like this one," waving vaguely toward the set, "and Lee's in it."

Honey nodded.

"Only she's not really in it. Her close-ups were cut in to match a different girl."

Honey's eyelids drooped at that one.

"I know why the film was faked: to extort money from Lee's stepmother. But it couldn't have been done without Lee's cooperation."

"You think the girl's holding up her mother?"

"It might seem that way."

"But you don't believe it. How come?"

"Doesn't fit. I meant it about Lee being a special person: almost otherworldly."

"And girls like that don't associate with dirty movies." There was no edge in Honey's soft, encouraging voice.

"That's not it; but girls like Lee don't blackmail their families."

Honey studied me thoughtfully, methodically kneading her cheeks and throat. Then she nodded. "What if Lee doesn't want to get found?"

"That's possible, but I'd like to make sure she's all right."

"And that she's as nice a girl as you think."

"That too, I guess."

Sighing, Honey dropped her hands in her lap. "You're better off not messing with it. I don't know anything myself, but I get a bad feeling about this place." She looked around her. Another sigh. "Well, I'll tell you where she's hiding: with some old gay guy up in the hills."

"Candy Wishbourne?"

"Don't gimme names, and don't you say I told you, hear?" Her drawl was creeping back in, as if she were retreating to her original distance. She stood up, stretching. "Look like Dolores is done fluffin' ol' Chuck, so I gotta clock back in to work."

Honey stood over me, knee to knee. From my seated position, she resembled the Venus of Willendorf. "You keep on keepin' on; but be sure you lookin' for the right thing in the right place."

The director said, "We're ready, Honey."

"Comin'." She looked at me for another beat, smiled gently again, then swung back toward the set.

The cast was busily reentangling as I quietly let myself out.

12

WHEEZING UP INTO THE TWILIT HOLLYWOOD HILLS toward Candy Wishbourne's I wanted a third eye to monitor
my rear-view mirror. But no vans behind so far, no traffic at
all on these semirural lanes. Streetlights were straggling on
erratically as their photocells decided independently when
it was indeed dark, while ten thousand insects set out tiny
sheet music and rosined their hind legs.

Candy's driveway was lined with cars tonight: Mercedes, Beetle, MG-TD, mini-pickup—and a flawless 1947
Packard resting on fat whitewalls by the front door.

Wrought-iron porch lamps splashed amber light on a
large red cross decorating the door. Party music floated out
the windows. I rang and waited.

The door was opened by a nurse out of a music hall
sketch: tiny cap riding a bouffant wig, double nose cone
bosom straining a uniform dress short enough to expose the
garters holding up white stockings. Spike-heeled pumps no
nurse could ever stand in.

"Well look who's here!" in a ringing basso. The "nurse"
was Herbie.

"Oh! Herbie; right. I'm Stoney Winston, remember? I
came to see Candy, but I guess I should have called first.
Having a party?"

Herbie focused, more or less, on a spot six inches in
front of me. "Having. A. Party. A rhetorical question, yes?
Or do you think I *always* dress this way?"

"Well no . . ."

"I'll bet you do. I'll bet you secretly do. *Think*, I mean,
not *dress*. Well why not?"

"Am I intruding?"

"I love intrusions. And extrusions. And protrusions. Come on in; show us your protrusion." Swinging the door wide, Herbie teetered toward the living room on his spike heels. I followed, doubtfully.

The dim living room continued the hospital motif. A bar was set out on a rolling gurney, complete with lab beakers for glasses. The ice bucket was a bedpan and other bedpans offered hors d'oeuvres. The all-male guests were costumed in lab coats, green surgical suits with paper shoe covers, or like Herbie, nurses' outfits. One reveler affected a patient gown which exposed his back and bottom. People talked in couples or small groups, or sat alone, immobilized in pharmaceutical recreations. There was pot too, from the smell.

Though bizarre, the effect was subdued or even dull, as if all the energy had been drained in carrying out the party theme, leaving none for the festivities themselves. I walked through suspended conversations and guarded looks, smiling politely, toward the chromium hospital bed against the opposite wall, on which Candy Wishbourne reclined, a fat odalisque in silk pajamas.

"Hey Candy."

"Ohmygod, look at *you*. Doctor Winston, I presume? Are you with someone? Why didn't you tell me? I never guessed."

"I'm alone."

"Where's your costume? You must have a costume or Herbie will throw you out on your tushie. No, just kidding—though he'd like to."

"What's the occasion?"

"I am, or more properly, my insides are. Yes, my Galens have consented to carve me up at last. Hospital tomorrow, surgery Monday, and out by the end of the week, right as a fiddle, fit as rain, big as a dollar. That's why they call doctors Hippocrits. Wait; a moment to consult my jug." Candy sucked on a length of surgical tubing attached to a hanging I.V. bottle, modified with glass lab equipment to make a water pipe. His eyes bulged and watered as he held the smoke down, then he whooshed marijuana fumes at me, coughing.

"Should you be smoking that?"

"Touching concern, dear man, but not to worry. Only booze is banned, you see; the issue being my liver. In more ways than one, I may say."

"I'm sure things will turn out for the best."

"Oh, *now* I get it: you came as Doctor Pangloss. Cute." Candy inhaled another lungful.

"Candy, I really came to see Lee Tolman. Where is she?"

"Where are the snows of yesteryear?"

"I know she's here; her friend Honey told me."

"You mean, 'her friend told me, *Honey*.' You're sweet too."

"Please, Candy. It's quite important."

"My attention has turned inward. I'm visualizing the shape of my pancreas." He siphoned out another toke of pot.

"Well, as long as I'm here, mind if I have a drink?"

Candy raised two plump arms to indicate the house was mine.

I mixed a weak, warm scotch, declining ice cubes from the bedpan, then settled my face in a blank, pleasant expression and wandered toward the kitchen. Herbie was bent over the oven, removing a cookie sheet of broiled cheese and crackers.

"Clever party, Herbie. Your idea?"

"Well, the concept. I mean, I couldn't really surprise him, could I? Besides, I didn't know where to rent all this shit." He waved the cookie sheet and one cracker skated off the edge to land on the stove.

I picked it up and ate it. "Good."

"I was going to serve nothing but liver: pâté, braunschweiger, rumaki—*you* know; but it seemed a bit much. Oh well."

"I understand. Say, where's the bathroom, Herbie?"

"Getting to you already? Down the hall."

I left him to lay out his crackers in a fresh bedpan.

I headed down the plastered, oak-beamed hall, pretending to search for the bathroom, cracking open doors set in deep recesses. Workroom filled with drafting table, blueprint cases, swing-arm lamp. Nope. Tiny den with a hugh projection TV at one end and a loveseat at the other, now occupied by a male couple giggling dreamily at a commercial. Master bedroom furnished in Early American: empty. Then the bathroom, which I didn't actually want to find, at least until I'd tried that last door down at the end of the hall.

It was locked. Knocking; waiting; waiting; knocking. No response. I knocked again.

"Go away." The voice was female.

"Lee?"

"Who is it?"

"Lee? I'm Stoney Winston. Can we talk?"

"No."

"Listen, I'm not—not a party guest." Silence. "I came to talk to you. Honey told me you were here."

"Honey?"

"At the studio. A black lady."

"Yes."

"She said you'd be here. Please, Lee; it's important for you."

"Why?"

"The film. It's gotten out of hand. I'm worried about you, Lee. Someone's dead."

Long pause, then, "Who's dead?" The door opened a crack. I couldn't see who was behind it.

"Who's dead?"

"I don't know—a woman. Can we talk?"

"Who are you?"

"Stoney Winston; I told you."

"I mean, where do you come in?"

"I was looking for you when I found the dead woman. I thought she was you."

The idea seemed to reach her. "Why would anyone want to kill me?"

"That's what I have to find out. Please, Lee."

Another long pause and then the door swung open. Lee Tolman scrutinized my face as if taking inventory, then dropped her eyes and stood back from the door.

No mistaking her: carrot hair, pale skin, oversized green eyes with almost invisible lashes, and a strange air of abstraction, as if much of her were simply elsewhere.

That weird, incorporeal beauty: the improbable spectral glow pulsing somehow, somewhere, inside. The face in the film was Lee's—no doubt about it.

But not the body. Standing there in cut-off shorts and pink T-shirt, her actual body was fuller-fleshed and bigger-boned, with strong, square feet and peasant ankles.

I felt obscurely betrayed by that thick form. The face that had floated so compelling above the slender movie body was now brought down to earth by a heavy load of sullen, stolid flesh. *My* Lee had been illusion—an editor's sleight-of-hand. This Lee was overweight and clunky.

She sat on the bed, still absorbed in her own thoughts, and I watched the shiny flesh tighten over fat as she flexed her knees. Her shoulders were plump as well, and her breasts were large and round—not the sloping cones I remembered from the film.

Memory stirred: something about breasts; then it slipped away. Just my residual prurience?

"Lee, I found a pornographic film. I thought you were in it. But I'm a film editor, and when I studied the work print, I saw that your close-ups were cut in later to match another . . . actress, to make it look as if you'd made the film. The fact is, you didn't."

She nodded, still staring at the rug.

"No one had seen you for two weeks, so I went looking. I found out about the Universal Church."

Lee's mouth wrinkled at the name.

"I thought you might be staying on a boat down at the marina, so I went looking for you there. I boarded the boat and searched it. There was a dead woman on the boat. I thought she was you."

Lee looked at me, puzzled.

"I couldn't see her face, but I recognized her body from your film." *One slack breast spilling out of her bikini top*. Breasts again, but what? . . . "I didn't know then that the film had been faked. You see why I thought it was you?"

Memory coming closer: pink foothills behind a scrim. Oh, no!

Lee got it simultaneously: "Peeper!"

"Yes. I just figured it out."

"Peeper's *dead*?" Her mouth dropped open and she swung her head in tiny, denying arcs. "No."

"Yes, Lee. The body belonged to the woman in the film."

"Peeper made that film with Jokie Driscoll."

"Then that was Peeper on Isiah Hammond's boat. Do you see why I thought you might be in trouble?"

"Why me?"

"I met your mother."

"She's not my mother."

"I mean your real mother, Ritchie Gershon. She told me about you and Hammond."

"That I slept with him? That's not 'in trouble.'"

"True, but Peeper *was*, and she was connected with Hammond, just like you."

"I don't think she slept with him."

"But she was killed on his boat. And because I found her, Hammond tried to have me killed too."

Lee stared at me, frowning, as if chasing down a fugitive thought. Then, "Yes, what about you? You never said where you fit in."

I sat down beside her, struggling to round up my own straying thoughts. There was no place to go without bringing up the extortion threat and Denise. Well, so be it.

She waited me out with eerie patience, until I'd assembled something to reply. "Denise Tolman hired me to find you because she wanted to suppress that film. The film bothered me, Lee, even before I realized it was faked. It didn't seem right. Your face was too . . . spiritual."

This corny word changed her. Lee looked at me in mild surprise and life flowed into her face. "Spiritual?"

"That's right: a beautiful, inward-looking quality. I couldn't square it with a dirty movie."

She actually looked animated.

"No one with such an inner light could have made that film."

Lee was nodding now in unison with my little hymn, and even as I mouthed this empty pap, I felt her uncanny power to transform it into truth. She had the gift of saints and demagogues: the ability to confer belief.

"Then I visited your mother in Ventura and she told me all about you. I think she loves you very much, Lee, but she's cut off." She looked pained at this. "Everything she said confirmed your . . . essential truth, your spiritual ambience." Though lacking all talent for these pieties, I sounded strangely sincere. I was starting to scare myself.

And Lee was still nodding. "I hoped Mama saw the truth. I tried to tell her."

"I know you feel a threat too. That's why you're hiding here."

"Not from Isiah."

"Who, then?"

"Not *who*." Her face closed slightly. "I thought you understood."

"I sometimes feel the truth before I understand it." She nodded again, as if this were logical. "Help me understand it."

Lee's personality disappeared, as if adjourning to an inner room. Then, after a lengthy introspection, she raised her two hands and inspected them, as if for cleanliness. "I don't know. I'll think about you."

"How do you mean?"

"I'll think. I trust my thoughts. But not tonight."

"Tomorrow, then?"

"I don't know."

"Let me come back tomorrow, please?" She stared at me calmly. "Please, Lee? It's important."

Finally: "Yes, it feels important. Yes."

"And stay here where it's safe."

"Yes."

"I'll come back tomorrow morning."

"Tomorrow." For the first time, Lee smiled.

Back down the hall toward the front of Candy's house. The living room orgy, if such it ever was, seemed more listless now than ever, with people standing or sitting dully. Candy an inert silk pile on his chrome bed. Herbie on the white piano stool, turning the nurse's wig in his hands as if puzzling over a small, hairy beast he'd trapped. In the provocative dress, with his own quarter-inch-long hair revealed, he resembled a caught collaborator, humiliated by the French Resistance.

13

Puffing clouds of smoke through the Sunday morning sunshine bouncing through my front windows from the patio, as I surrendered to an occasional craving: a cheap cigar. I pretended this ten-cent cheroot was a sweet Havana corona and the puffer was my mentor, Sigmund Freud.

His small, neat feet paced out a tidy pattern as he talked. "Regarding Fraulein Tolman, the picture you present is inconsistent."

"That shouldn't surprise you, Doctor."

"Nothing surprises me." Unhitching circular spectacles, he scrubbed them with a dazzling hankie. "But you are, as an observer, an amateur at best." Freud peered into a corner, as if surveying a full lecture hall.

"Consider . . ."

"I'm over here."

"Ach." He reinstalled his spectacles; revolved: "Ah! Why have you this need to be elusive?"

"We were discussing Lee Tolman."

"Lee Tolman, *ja*. Let me see: the subject displays a profound spirituality. . . ."

"I don't know how profound."

"Please! A profound spirituality manifesting itself in a quest for inner fulfillment; a quest leading her—I should even say *driving* her—to a succession of sects of more or less doubtful respectability."

"Crackpots, the lot."

My mentor winced. "There are no *crackpots*, Herr Winston; only people in some measure disordered." Three aggressive puffs shrank Freud's corona a full inch. "This

131

hunger for spirituality has rendered the subject vulnerable
to predators such as Isiah Hammond."

"Are you sure the hunger's purely spiritual?"

"One is sure, in my profession, of nothing. But you
have put the finger on an inconsistency. The subject displays, as it were simultaneously, a suppressed but powerful
sensuality."

"That's how I saw it."

"This is not surprising. But even making allowances for
your own considerable libido, your perception is probably
accurate. This ashtray is overflowing. Why do you feel so
reluctant to part with your ashes?"

"I think of them as cigar shit."

Sudden twinkle behind the round black frames. "I cannot be shocked, Herr Winston."

"Nor abbreviated, apparently. You're not addressing
my problem."

Icicles formed on Freud's reply: "State it."

My turn to pace through the smoke cloud. "I need information from Lee and I don't know how to pry it out of
her."

"Explain, please."

"If she's extorting money from Denise, she's not going
to tell *me* about it."

"*Vielleicht*, but when last night you spoke with her, she
tacitly admitted making those close-ups."

"Tacitly. Then there's the Hammond business."

"She admitted this relationship as well."

"But she didn't seem to know what Peeper Martin was
doing on Hammond's boat. Until I get that mess sorted out,
I'm not safe."

Freud steepled dainty fingers, making his cigar resem-
ble a cannon protruding from a teepee—a dubious image,
considering. "Let us discuss these fears of yours."

"Let us get on with Lee Tolman. I'm consulting you
because you're renowned for digging information out of
people. Now what questions should I ask?"

A disdainful wave. "It hardly matters. I ask very few questions, Herr Winston. Instead, I listen and listen and listen. Eventually, I hear answers."

"And *eventually* can be profitable at eighty bucks an hour."

The patrician face assumed a wistful look. "So much? How times have changed." The lecture resumed: "Here is my prescription: Fraulein Tolman is out, as you would put it, to lunch. But she is neither hypocritical nor stupid. So: do not repeat your wretched performance of last evening."

"My? . . ."

"Your bleatings about 'spirituality' and 'inner qualities.' These insincerities will not long deceive her."

"That's the weird part: I *wasn't* insincere."

Freud inspected that with therapeutic distrust, then resumed his train of thought.

"Instead, win her confidence by prompting *her* to talk."

"And how do I do that?"

Freud retreated into his Cuban smog. "Listening, Herr Winston, is remarkably effective. One day, you must try it." Only a glint of lenses now; then they too disappeared.

Not much advice on extracting confessions. I should have consulted Torquemada.

Into my wardrobe department for a nonjudgmental costume. A golf shirt, I think, and my virgin sneakers: laces intact, toes unsmudged, Sears' indifferent best. A brief appointment with my razor, then out to charm the pants off Lee Tolman.

A ghostly chuckle signaled Freud's return. "Interesting, Herr Winston: you speak, unconsciously, of removing pants. Next session, we will explore your self-delusions. A subject of considerable scope, *nicht wahr*?"

I rang Candy Wishbourne's doorbell, knowing vaguely what I wanted to achieve, but still without a clue on how to do it.

The spy hole in the door opened to reveal Lee's astonishing green eye. "Is that you, uh? . . ."

"Stoney Winston, yes."

"I forgot your name. Herbie took Candy to the hospital this morning."

"May I come in?"

Framed in the little opening, her disembodied eye resembled an occult symbol. "I thought about you last night." I waited. The eye shifted to inspect my sternum. "About Peeper too."

"Did you think about the danger?"

"I don't feel any, no."

"Then how about letting me in?"

"I'm coming out. I'm on my way to church."

The *chunk* of a deadbolt withdrawing, then the door opened and Lee emerged, dressed in running shoes, shorts, and a tank top.

"Church?"

"I think of it that way. Want to see?" She started up the steep driveway in heavy, solid strides. Like the composite girl in the film, Lee appeared to be two different people: an ethereal head mismatched to an earthbound body.

I pulled the front door shut and followed her up to the road.

We strolled along together in the hard September sunlight, inhaling dust and scrubby smells, inspecting the olive, tan, and yellow hills. A pair of hawks spiraled above us in endless, patient patrol. Lee said nothing. Soon the terrain grew too steep for even extravagant Hollywood builders and the stilt-top houses petered out into open country. Here Lee left the hot asphalt and started up into a tiny canyon full of crackling grass. The faint path twisted until the road below was out of sight.

The canyon dead-ended in a miniature amphitheater filled with a huddle of live oak trees, hiding away as if to conceal their precious source of underground water. Lee dropped at the foot of a gnarled trunk and crossed her legs in lotus position.

"I see what you mean about your church."

She nodded, then sat absolutely motionless, green eyes focused at infinity.

Nothing to do but wait her out. I lay back and played at meditating: recite my secret whatsit, clear the psychic tubes, empty the mind.

Empty, the stomach; wish I'd had breakfast. Concentrate.

Full, the bladder too. Come on; leave the mundane behind.

Amazing how the tiny stones beneath you grow to boulders as you lie on them.

To hell with it.

By wagging my head slightly, I could make the sunlight scamper back and forth among the dark leaves above me. Nice little effect. Remember it the next time I'm filming.

Half mesmerized by the hot sparkles, I almost missed what Lee was saying.

"I come here to experience totality."

Long silence.

"Complete wholeness."

More silence.

"Can't you feel it?"

"In a way. But this is your place, Lee. That's why you feel it more."

"My place. I hope so; I've tried so many."

"What happened?"

"People, mainly. I guess I expect too much."

I was about to weigh in with something pompous when I remembered Freud's warning. Instead: "People like Hammond?"

"Hatred is so degrading; but I don't hate him any more."

"Why did you hate Hammond?"

"It wasn't the screwing." The phrase sounded strangely innocuous in her gentle, faraway tone. "There are many roads to oneness and the body travels one of them."

That sounded like a maxim she'd read. I played with the sparkles some more, waiting.

"Did you know Peeper was a redhead like me?"

"Between her wigs and makeup, I couldn't tell. Why did you think of that?"

"I hated Isiah and that caused Peeper to die. I thought about it last night."

"Well . . ."

"This is how it happened. I met Isiah Hammond at the studio and he touched me and I felt a teacher in him."

Cross-legged before the dappled tree trunk, amid the dust and buzzing bugs, she told her story in long, formal cadences, like a holy man rolling out a favorite parable: how she'd introduced herself to Hammond and questioned him about Things Spiritual; how kind he'd been and patient; how he'd offered her a job and how fulfilled she'd been working for him; how their rapport had grown and how, at length, in a natural convergence of body and spirit, they had become completely one. How in time, another woman had caught Hammond's eye and how he had replaced Lee as offhandedly as if he were discarding a slightly frayed suit.

All this was recited in the quaint, distant language of a folk tale, once upon a time. Hard to tell whether this was to protect herself against the memory, or just the way Lee Tolman saw reality.

I moved over beside her and crossed my own legs self-consciously. "I can see why you hated Hammond."

She looked at me blankly, as if emerging from a trance; then she frowned. "I did; and I hated hating him. It set me back years."

"How so?"

"I thought I'd grown beyond that."

"How did the film come into all this?"

"Mr. Nahan. It was his idea."

I concealed my astonishment.

"He found me at the studio after I . . . well, I guess I ran away from the church. I said some things to Isiah and he was ugly and I was very upset. And Mr. Nahan came and

found me. He told me how worried he was about me—
about how unhappy I must be. He talked about how degrading it was and how he couldn't keep Isiah from doing
this to girls. He was very distressed because the church is
his whole life."

Nahan? This sounded like another fairytale of Lee's.

"I felt sorry for him and I felt so . . . frustrated that I
couldn't do anything about it."

"Then what happened?"

"Well, Mr. Nahan said he had a plan. He didn't want
me to get the wrong idea or anything, but he knew the kind
of movies Pepe made at the studio. He wanted me to make
one so he could use it on Isiah."

"A pornographic movie? Nahan?"

"I was so surprised. I mean, how could he even think of
such a thing?"

"How did he plan to use the film?"

"He wasn't very clear. He talked about telling Isiah to
stop taking advantage of people like me or else he'd show
the film I guess—or something."

"He wasn't too specific."

"I didn't let him. I said right away I could never make
one of those movies."

"Then what?"

"Well, Peeper had an idea."

"Where did she come in?"

"I went to the studio to find her. I thought maybe I
could stay with her for a while. But she helps Pepe make
those movies and she said why didn't Mr. Nahan use one of
her films, because she and I are both redheads."

"But aside from your coloring, you don't look alike."

"That's what Mr. Nahan said. So Peeper explained how
Pepe could take pictures of just my head and shoulders and
put me in Peeper's film. That way, I wouldn't have to . . . do
anything. I don't really understand how it works."

She sifted dust through her fist. "I still didn't like it,
but Mr. Nahan said I'd be like an actress doing a professional job. To make it just business, he'd even pay me five

hundred dollars. He talked about how Isiah threw me out and didn't give me my last paycheck and so it would only be fair. And I didn't have any money or any place to stay."

"Peeper wouldn't put you up?"

"No. And I kept thinking how Isiah pretended to me and how he used me and I hated him. So I said all right."

"How did they shoot your part of the film?"

"We did it on that set they use all the time. I laid down on the bed and Pepe pulled my shirt down off my shoulders. He told me when to lie on my stomach and when to turn over. He wanted me to wiggle and smile, but I didn't do it very well."

I recalled the close-ups of Lee's serene face. "What happened to the film?"

"I don't know. I didn't want to see it."

I leaned against the knobby oak, counting improbabilities: Nahan just happened to find Lee at the studio and Peeper just happened to be there. Nahan knew all about Pepe's porn operation and had a ready-made plan to exploit it. When Lee was reluctant to make a dirty movie, Peeper—poor simple Peeper—came up with the sophisticated plan of faking the film using inserts that exploited the slight resemblance between the two redheaded women. Pepe was only too happy to dress and light a set, shoot the inserts, and cut in the results—just like that. And Pepe knew the original film well enough to shoot perfectly matched close-ups.

Sure.

Nahan, Pepe, and Peeper had obviously worked the whole plan out beforehand and set Lee up.

But not to blackmail Hammond. Nahan was far too sharp for such a lamebrained scheme. And not to extort money from Denise. Nahan was skimming the church of more than fifty thousand a month—and with less risk.

I faced the possibility that Lee was fabricating all this, to cover the fact that she herself was holding up her stepmother.

"Lee, what's the trouble between you and Denise?"

At the name, Lee shrugged and lay back on the matted yellow weeds. "Nothing. We just never got very close. She has her house and her garden and her—*things*. I don't care about things. She doesn't care about—"

"Values?"

"Yes; so I can't relate to her. But she's a nice person."

"Where does Candy Wishbourne come in?"

"I hope he's all right. He's very sick."

"I hope he's all right too. How did you end up staying with him?"

"I felt he was a kind man." For her, that was reason enough.

"Why do you think Peeper was on Hammond's boat?"

"I liked sailing: sun, water, sky; you're like a dot at the center of everything." She sat up. "But Isiah only took me once."

"And Peeper?"

"I don't know. Maybe he met her at the studio too."

Lee rose and stretched, lifting her tank top clear of her shorts. Un-self-conscious as a child, she scratched her pink stomach.

"I better go back. Herbie said he'd call from the hospital." She clomped down the steep trail with oddly awkward steps. I followed her through the dusty yellow glare down to the road.

Trying to drive the Rabbit home without quite touching the seat, which had reached the temperature of a well-done roast. I cursed the sadists who upholster California cars in black plastic. Hollywood lay deserted in the hot Sunday afternoon, torpid as a snake on a rock.

I walked down the steps beside Sally's house and around to my door, which had blown open. Must do better about locking things; Laurel Canyon's alive with felons.

Out of the dazzle and into my dark cave.

"Get him!" This in the wheezy tenor yip of a fat lapdog, from a thick shape in the center of my living room. My arms were grabbed and twisted behind me. The murky image resolved into the familiar fat man, still in his lumberjack shirt, still with a gun in his paw.

He stared at me, blinking as if I'd disrupted his hibernation. "Gotta good hold?"

The grip on my arms tightened. "Yeah."

The fat man scratched his scruffy beard. "Hello, asshole."

"What do you want?"

"Already got it. You sonofabitch, you know what you did to the side of my truck? Goddam fire engine like to run me off the road."

"Talk to my insurance broker."

Another long, blinking stare, then: "I'll tell him about my nose too." The fat man's nose was the size and shape of a small beet and nearly the same color. "We got to settle for that."

"As long as Bonzo holds my arms."

Another pause, as if the fat man processed ideas with painful effort. "Uh-uh, not here. Too loud for this nice neighborhood. Okay, tie him up."

"What with?" The voice behind me belonged to the tall man.

The fat man shook his head and sighed. "Aw Earl, *find* something. I'll cover him."

Releasing me, the tall man disappeared into the kitchen. Silence, except for cupboard doors banging off-screen. The fat man sighed again, but kept his eyes on me.

The tall man returned. "Nothin' there."

"Use his belt."

"We got rope in the van."

"Don't leave. Use his belt."

"Okay." The tall man crossed in front of me to reach the buckle. I tensed.

"Get outta there, Earl; you're blocking me. Make *him* take it off." The tall man backed up hastily.

"Stoney?" Sally's voice from outside the house.

The fat man jerked the gun up to keep me silent, but I wasn't about to call out. Go away, Sally; get lost.

"Hey Stoney, I need some help."

Go *away*, Sally. Three seconds of dead silence.

The door pushed open and Sally started in. "I was sunbathing on the deck. Got my bra all . . ." Two steps inside, she froze, gaping at the sight of the two men and the gun. She was in a bikini bottom, her left arm holding a towel across her chest, her right one behind the towel.

Sally goggled. "Hey!"

"Shut up. Get in here."

Her mouth dropped open as she stared at the fat man. "Hey, is that a *gun?*" As if stupefied by the sight, she let her arms slide downward until her big breasts bounced clear. "What is this, Stoney? What's going on?"

It was the thin man's turn to gape. "Jesus Christ, willya look at—"

Sally dropped the towel completely and snapped into a police academy crouch, aiming a .38 special two-handed: "*Freeze, sucker!*"

The barked command, the half-nude woman, and the big pistol overloaded the fat man's circuits. I charged him, snatched at his gun hand, wrenched it up. Deafening noise as he fired into the ceiling. I tried to wrestle the gun away but he jerked his thick arm clear and swung on me.

Another numbing explosion. The fat man screamed and collapsed. I stomped on his gun hand and he screamed again. I grabbed his gun and swung around, but Sally had the tall man cowering before her .38.

"Sit!" she commanded, and doglike, the tall man sat on the floor beside his whimpering partner, trying to avoid the blood spreading over my carpet. The fat man was holding his thigh and blubbering. "Jesus, I'm losing blood. Jesus. For God's sake."

"Quiet! Tie it off, Stoney. Use your belt, like the man suggested."

I looped the belt around a thigh as big as my waist and cinched it tight. "Here: you hold it." The fat man grabbed at the belt tongue.

"Better call the police, Stoney."

I hesitated, then an idea occurred to me. I walked out the front door and closed it behind me, then kicked at the panel until the cheap snap lock splintered out of the wood and the door swung wide. Reentering, I wagged the fat man's gun at the shattered door.

"I know we all want to keep things simple, gents, so when the police get here, you can take your choice: ordinary breaking and entering or attempted murder. What's your feeling?"

The tall man glanced over at the fat man, who was rocking back and forth, eyes squeezed shut in pain. "What's he mean?"

The fat man nodded. "Shut up, Earl. Okay okay, just call willya? I gotta get a doctor."

"A simple burglary attempt, correct?"

"Yeah."

"All right, on your faces. Fast!" The tall man obediently lay prone. The fat man whimpered, "I can't hold it that way."

"Tough. Put your hands between your legs and grab the belt. Move!"

Groaning, the fat man heaved over until he was lying with his arms underneath him and his face in his blood.

"And I'll tell the Reverend Hammond you've left his employ."

The fat man's whine was muffled. "Whaterya talking about?"

"I think you know."

I phoned the police to explain that we had cornered two burglars and one of them was slightly wounded. No, we were all right; my lady friend shot him with a pistol. The police asked *what* pistol.

"That's right, Sally; where'd you get the gun?"

"I keep it in my night table. Didn't you know that? I bought it when the house next door was robbed. Even took a course at a firing range."

I explained this to the law and they promised to come right out.

"Sally, how did you know? . . ."

She waved at the prone figures and shook her head.

"All right, but do me a favor, please?"

"What?"

"Before the cops arrive, put a top on."

Standing at the sink in Sally's kitchen, solving the nightly puzzle of the dishwasher. Plastic on the top rack, wine glasses kept upside down by adjacent coffee mugs, cooking spoons wedged to keep them from slipping through the bottom rack and stopping the sprayer arm. Well done; I've always been good at packing. I pushed the button.

"Why do you run rinse-and-hold when it's almost full?" Dish cloth in hand, Sally stared with honest puzzlement.

Piously: "Running a full load saves energy."

"Oh Stoney, get serious. Rinse-and-hold burns energy too." She free-associated from my keen domestic insights: "Why do you want to get married?"

A pause while I scrambled to shift gears. I watched a visiting cat (one of scores in the neighborhood) heft a piece of chicken carcass from the kitchen floor, before transferring it to the living room carpet.

"Just keep it off the couch this time, cat."

"Earth to Stoney: *why do you want to get married?* How is it better when it's official?"

"It's not 'better.' " A long pause so silent I could hear the cat pounding across the vinyl tiles. "Why buy instead of leasing? Why plant seeds?" My bromides clanked like plastic chimes. "I sound like *Readers' Digest*."

Sally scrubbed a roasting pan. Faint munchings floated in from the living room. The pan approached surgical standards for asepsis.

She addressed the pan in a small, odd voice: "Trite but true." Ostentatious change of subject: "Big day today."

"I loved the way you stunned them with your chest."

"I'd like to take the credit, but I never thought of that part."

"What made you get your gun and come downstairs?"

"I was sunbathing on the deck and fell fast asleep. When I woke up, I looked over the rail and there was a van parked way down around the far corner of the house—as if it was hiding. Then I remembered what you said about those two men and a van. So I grabbed the pistol out of my night table and snuck down. When I heard them talk about tying you up, I knew who they were."

"I wish you hadn't taken the risk."

"Look who's talking." Putting her hands on her hips, Sally stared blankly at the sink. "You know, it's funny: I felt *good*, a rush, a tingle—like skydiving or sex. You want a beer?"

"The law was a bit nonplussed at your prowess."

"I told them about practicing at the firing range."

I started my bottle of Dos Equis Dark. "You know, kicking my door in means I can never go to the police."

"About the dead girl."

"I'd have to admit I lied about those men."

"You're in no deeper than before."

"And with those characters put away, I can move around safely."

"I'd still be careful." Sally paused, as if to choose words carefully. Then a facial shrug and, "I'll take the trash out."

14

Downhill all the way from Laurel Canyon to Denise's studio, fortunately for my wheezing Rabbit, driven to near-collapse by the past week's exertions.

It couldn't have been a whole week. But it had been Monday when I was summomed from my cozy prop house hideout to chase a dirty movie and now it was Monday once again.

I chugged past the glitzy stucco flats lining Hollywood Boulevard. Pedestrians in funny-looking clothes watered funnier-looking dogs.

Maybe it's the lack of weather here: same kiln-baked sky, same sauna heat, same yellow blare day after day. Or maybe it's because everything's happened so quickly: Peeper killed, Lee lost and found, the movie puzzle solved.

But not solved completely, which is why I was bound for another chat with Señor Pepe.

Pepe's costume upheld his customary standard: white Dacron safari jacket over purple shirt, black pants, and white leather loafers that cunningly simulated plastic.

He finger-combed his mustache with twitchy hands. "Make this fast, my friend."

"I'm not your friend, Pepe, but I'll do you a favor anyway."

Pepe did an eyebrow trick he must have practiced in a mirror. Leaning toward him suddenly, I plucked the purple kerchief from his breast pocket.

"Hey!"

I polished a corner of his desk, then sat on it and flipped the purple cloth into his wastebasket. "As you say, let's make it fast. You'll need time to tidy up before the police arrive."

He froze, bent over with his hand half-way to the wastebasket, then straightened in his desk chair with studied calm.

"You've been making pornographic films here, Pepe, probably with underage actresses."

"This is your story."

"Without your employer's knowledge and consent. Now she knows."

He picked at his mustache. "Mrs. Tolman . . ."

". . . Will doubtless fire you, but that's the least of your troubles. One of your films was used to blackmail Mrs. Tolman. Would you care to discuss it? It featured Jokie Driscoll, Peeper Martin—and Lee Tolman."

"I know nothing of it."

"Of course not, despite the fact that you lit, shot, and edited the inserts to make it look as if Lee was in the original movie."

"I—"

"Lee told me how you did it."

"Lee?"

"I found her. Nice of you to let the boss' daughter hang around. She knows a lot about your operation."

"And she has told this to the police?"

"Just the dirty movies, not the blackmail."

Pepe ventured a smirk, which I cut short: "Then there's the matter of Peeper's murder."

"What?!"

"Nice little reaction, Pepe; too bad I wasn't shooting your close-up. You know perfectly well that Peeper's skull was squashed and her body dumped in the Catalina Channel."

"No!"

"Yes! And I'm betting you know exactly how it happened."

"I have not seen her since last week, but—"

"Sure. We're making it fast, remember? So let's get right to it. The police don't know about your connection with Peeper and they don't know about the blackmail—yet. So you and I are going to trade silences."

"I do not see what this means."

"I'll take it slowly, Pepe; watch my lips. Mrs. Tolman is a prominent citizen in Pasadena and it would embarrass her to have her daughter's naughty joke made public."

"I see."

"Of course you see; that's why you blackmailed her to begin with."

"It was Peeper's idea."

"Everyone accuses Peeper of ideas. Poor Peeper; whatever brains she had are fish meal now."

Pepe looked grey. "I cannot believe it."

"Nice try. To the police, Peeper's just another dead Jane Doe—so far. And she'll stay that way as long as you keep quiet about Lee's film."

A pause while he did some heavy thinking. Pepe didn't know who really killed Peeper, but he would want no truck with the law. From his point of view, this would be a useful trade. Finally, he nodded.

"Give me the whole story. What did Wilton Nahan have to do with the film?"

"That bastard; it was his idea. He said we could make some money off Hammond."

"How?"

"He had some pictures of Hammond with Lee Tolman. They were innocent things—snapshots or something. But they showed Hammond was connected with this girl."

"Go on."

Pepe shrugged. "I do not know. Nahan *said* if people found out that Hammond's woman was a whore, it would ruin him with the church."

"So you made her a whore with a little movie magic."

"Nahan said he would pretend to receive the film in the mail from some unknown persons. 'They' would ask for money. Nahan would tell Hammond to pay it. Peeper and I, we would get half." Pepe reached absently for his handkerchief, remembered, retrieved it from his wastebasket. He blew his nose.

"What happened?"

"Nada! Nahan said Hammond refused to pay. But I know that Nahan. He got the money and kept it all."

"But he gave you an idea: why not try the same thing on Denise Tolman?"

"She could afford it."

I stood up. "All right."

"What about the police?"

I pretended to consider, then: "All they know is that you made some dirty movies. They'll try to nail you at it, so you better shut down. Strike that set; clean out the cutting room. Without evidence, they can't do much." Pepe brightened slightly. "Then conduct business as usual."

"Hah! What business?"

"Just remember our bargain: you keep quiet about the film and I keep quiet about Peeper."

"But I know nothing about her!"

"You were partners in two different blackmail schemes and a porno operation. How's that going to look?"

"It is not fair."

"Peeper would doubtless agree."

I was swinging around to go when Pepe actually plucked me by the sleeve: "With no kidding, Winston, she is really dead?" I nodded.

Pepe's face showed the only genuine feeling I'd ever seen on it. He turned his head away.

I dog-trotted down the stairs from Pepe's office and out to stumpy Gladys in the studio lobby.

"Gladys, my dear, I have a confession."

Gladys leered at the only man who still flirts with her. "I'll be gentle with you, Stoney."

"I'm coming out of the closet."

A wail: "Not *you!*"

"Wrong closet. I've been hanging around here for a reason. I know how you feel about Pepe, so I think I can trust you."

Gladys' eyes lit up with healthy malice.

"Pepe's up to something funny. Denise Tolman hired me to snoop around and find out what it is."

"Creative accounting?"

"Maybe more, but I haven't found enough. So just now, I went to Pepe and lit a fire under him."

"That's a happy thought."

"Now I need to find out how he reacts. Does the whole studio share the same phone lines?"

"Sure: oh-six-five through six-nine." She fingered the buttons on her desk phone.

"Including Pepe?"

Gladys looked positively radiant: "I've got the message."

"*All* the messages, coming in or out. Can you pick up his line without getting caught?"

"I've been a studio secretary for twenty years. What do *you* think?"

"You have my home number? Good. At worst, you get to talk to my machine. Now I've got to do some running about."

"Be careful, Stoney; take care of that bod."

"Love you too, Gladys."

I nursed the Rabbit up into the Hollywood hills, en route to Candy Wishbourne's to cross-check Pepe's story with Lee Tolman, particularly one false note: cheap extortion was not Nahan's style. Besides, milking the church was far too profitable to bother with blackmail.

Bouncing onto the remote, half-rural road to Candy's house, I spotted a coyote padding toward me along the shoulder, driven out of the scrub in search of water. He looked as seedy as his cartoon counterpart.

Herbie's yellow eye appeared behind the spy hole in Candy's door.

"Stoney Winston, Herbie; can I see Lee Tolman?"

Sullen answer muffled by the door: "Not here."

"Could you tell me where she is?"

"No."

"Do you know?"

"Go away."

"If Lee isn't here, she may be in trouble. Please!"

The yellow eye consulted heaven in annoyance, but then the tiny door closed and a lengthy rigmarole of clanks and rattles followed. The door swung open.

"What?"

Herbie's costume was surprising: slacks and sober jacket and a tie. He'd even removed the gold stud from his earlobe. "I'm leaving for the hospital."

"How is Candy?"

"They started at seven. It's been five hours now. I phone every hour but I get the same runaround, so I'm going down there."

"I won't keep you, but I do have to find Lee."

"She left."

"When?"

"I didn't notice."

"Could I just check her room?"

A sigh. "Make it fast." He stood aside.

All traces of the party had vanished, leaving the living room and tiny hall immaculate. As I started down the corridor, the phone rang and Herbie scampered into the living room.

Lee's bedroom had been cleaned out: no clothes in the closet, no toiletries in the connecting bath, no suitcase. I walked back into the living room.

I started to ask if the caller was Lee, but the sight of Herbie stopped me. He stood with the receiver dangling from one hand, tears leaking down his sparrow face. A dial tone floated out of the telephone, unnaturally loud. I took the receiver out of his hand and hung it up. He looked at me without expression, still weeping.

"Candy?"

He nodded, swallowing.

"What happened?"

Herbie shook his head several times, staring at the carpet.

"Come in the kitchen." I led him there by the elbow. "Here, sit down." Shaking his head again, he leaned against a counter. "Want a drink, Herbie?"

"I stopped drinking so *he* wouldn't . . ." Herbie's voice failed. He cleared his throat and looked around the cheery kitchen.

"The surgeon said they opened Candy up and he was a terrible mess inside. They thought if they could cut most of it out, he might have a little time." Another head shake. "But he started hemorrhaging and they couldn't stop it."

"I'm very sorry."

"They're lying. The could have stopped the blood."

"I'm sure they tried."

"I think they meant to be kind. When they saw how bad he was, they let him go gracefully."

"What do you have to do now?"

"Candy did everything. Before he . . . left, he put out the insurance, his will, deed to the house, taxes. He was so tidy; he even left a note about the car payment." Herbie kept control of his face but his eyes were filling again.

I tried to head him off. "Well, he was luckier than many: he had someone who loved him."

Herbie saw I'd meant that very simply. He nodded a hint of thanks.

"Herbie, I know this is the worst possible time to bother you, but Lee Tolman is in real danger. You and Candy sort of looked after her together, so I know you'd like to help."

His shrug asked how.

"Try to think where she might have gone."

He wiped his brimming eyes with the heel of a hand, thinking. "She didn't get any phone calls."

"Did she talk about anything with you?"

"We had supper last night. I fixed deviled eggs. We didn't say much. Then she started talking about going back; returning to the source; finding the beginning; that kind of thing. I didn't follow half of it."

"Back where?"

"She didn't actually say."

"Thanks, Herbie. Again, I'm very sorry about Candy." Herbie nodded.

Twisting back down to Hollywood, full of mortal thoughts. Fat friendly Candy dead; Herbie forlorn. Grotesque image of Peeper's sad leavings.

And now maybe Lee, after all. She was just strange enough to confront Hammond with her knowledge that he killed Peeper.

I had to find Hammond—at least to make sure Lee wasn't with him.

Back in my apartment, I perfected a suitably Old Testament voice before phoning Hammond's office.

"Reverend Hammond hasn't come in today."

In my most resonant tones, "And when do you expect him, young lady?"

"He'll be in before tonight's telecast."

"I see. This is Reverend Randall Samples of the Gardena Assembly of God. It's about a donation to our churches."

A pause on the other end of the line. Better up the ante: "A very large donation."

"Well . . . he's usually home around supper time."

"In Beverly Hills?"

"Mount Hyperion, actually. But I can't give out his phone number."

"Thank you; I'll call again."

Mount Hyperion Estates: two dozen mansions behind a high wall with a security gate house. Wait a minute: Sam Graffman lives there—the producer. Into my black book for his phone number.

"Graffman residence." The British tones of Andrew the major domo—too lower-class for an Old Country Jeeves, but the colonials don't know the difference.

"Andy, this is Stoney Winston. How are you?"

"My dear Winston: blimey!" Andrew enhances his local image with antique British slang. "Are you working for the old boy again?"

"Not this time. I need help with a location problem."

"Delighted to oblige."

"I'm looking for an estate and I remembered that place the preacher lives in—you know, Isiah Hammond?"

"That vulgar thing with the Greek columns?"

"Right. How far up from you is it?"

"Just three houses. But you can't shoot in Mount Hyperion."

"No?"

"Oh no; they'd never let you."

"Too bad. Well, it was just a thought. Thanks, Andy."

"Always a pleasure, old boy."

Knowing half the noncoms in Hollywood comes in handy.

Into the wardrobe department for a civil servant costume: my only suit, white shirt, and a not quite fashionable tie sent by Mama six Noels back. The effect was passable.

I consulted the household prop resources for a pocket notebook and ballpoint pen, plus two octagonal film shipping cases from my editing supplies. Up to Sally's bedroom to retrieve the .38 pistol from her night table.

Then off to Hollywood Props Incorporated to hire a shoulder holster and a plausible police ID. I hid the holster, tie, and jacket on the Rabbit's floorboards and placed the film shipping cans prominently on the seat beside me. Then westward down Sunset Boulevard toward Mount Hyperion Estates, preparing two roles at once: first a studio delivery man; then a plodding minion of the law.

15

Twilight was approaching as I corkscrewed up the outer approach to Mount Hyperion and stopped at the pretentious gate house, to confront a guard wearing a banana republic uniform complete except for medals.

"Hi! Got a print here for Mr. Graffman. He's going to project it tonight."

"You gotta call."

"I know." I bounced into the kiosk, friendly as a puppy. "Let's see: he's three-oh-eight, right?"

"Yeah."

I punched in the numbers; waited.

"Graffman residence." A maid answered, sparing me the need to explain a second call to Andy.

"I have a print here—for Mr. Graffman's screening?"

"Wait a minute. I'll ask about it."

Talking to the now abandoned phone: "Okay, I'll bring it right up." To the guard: "All set."

"Know the house?"

"Oh sure."

"Never seen you here before."

"The regular driver told me."

"Sign in."

I scribbled "Harry Secombe/Sellers Enterprises" and hopped back in the Rabbit, praying the maid wouldn't phone the guard when she returned to a disconnected call.

Up the long, looping road in the near-dark, past five or six architectural extravaganzas, past the Graffman's silent pile, past two more homes, to a looming Doric fantasy set well back from the road: the Reverend Hammond's cozy parish cottage.

154

Up a gravel drive so white it must be dusted daily; I parked as inconspicuously as the lemon-colored Rabbit allowed. Two minutes to install shoulder holstered gun, lash up necktie, and don jacket. Several deep breaths while I practiced thinking like a TV cop, then up to the big paneled door.

"Yea-uh?" in the resonant drawl of Isiah Hammond, who had opened the door himself.

"Reverend Hammond? I'm Sam Bagdassarian, L.A.P.D." I was quoting the name on the prop ID, which I removed from my jacket pocket and flashed one-handed, very professionally, so that Hammond had almost enough time to read it. "Like to ask a couple questions."

"What about?"

"May I come in, sir?"

"I guess." He held the door while I strolled past him into the foyer, which I surveyed calmly, like a cop who looks at everything.

"Is there someplace we can talk quietly, sir?"

"Well . . . the living room. Don't I know you?"

"Yes sir, I took a statement from you at your studio on . . ." consulting pocket notebook, ". . . Thursday of last week at 1:43 PM." Flipping the notebook shut. "I was working undercover at that time."

The living room was Beverly Hills Decorator, all busy fabrics and plants distributed as if to dress a set.

"I do recall you. About the Tolman child."

"Lee Tolman, yes sir. As I stated at that time, Miss Tolman was missing. She still is."

"I am sorry for her poor folks' worry."

"Yes sir. Can you tell me your whereabouts between the hours of two and eight PM on that Thursday?"

Hammond reached in the neck of his expensive polo shirt to scratch his chest hair. "I believe I should know what this is all about."

"You are the owner of the cutter *Mixed Blessing*, is that correct, sir?"

"What's that got to do with anything?"

"At approximately six PM on that date, I discovered a deceased body aboard the vessel."

"A *what*?!"

"A female Caucasian aged twenty to twenty-five, approximately five feet-six, light complexion, red hair."

"Not *Lee*?"

"No sir. Subsequent investigation revealed that the victim was a Miss Martin, nickname Peeper."

Hammond looked genuinely confused. "Who? . . ."

"Upon discovering the body, I attempted to exit the vessel, but ascertained that I was locked in. When I did emerge through a hatch, I was set upon and thrown overboard." A meaningful stare at Hammond. "I believe you recognized me at that time, sir."

"I wasn't even there!"

"As I continued my undercover investigation, I was twice attacked by two individuals in your employ."

Hammond's confusion was shading into worry. "Two? . . ."

"Up to that point in time, my efforts were focused on certain financial activities connected with your church. But since the alleged murder of Miss Martin, I've been cooperating with Homicide Division. It would save time, sir, if you'd cooperate too."

"What financial activities? Listen, I do not have to respond to you."

I put my hands on my hips, drawing back my jacket to display the shoulder holster as I nodded with patient resignation. "All right, Reverend, I guess we better go downtown." Flipping to the front of my notebook, I pretended to read a Miranda Card in a bored drone: "You-have-the-right-to-remain-silent-you . . ."

"Now hold the phone; let's just start right over again. Firstly, I have not been on that boat in more'n a week."

"What about the date in question, sir?"

"Thursday?" Hammond thought, then brightened. "I was, uh, with a certain lady."

"Her name, sir?"

"Lisa Torres." In Hammond's drawl, the name came out "Leeza Torse." "She does makeup at the studio. We went to lunch an', well . . ."

"Where?"

"Harold's Steak House, on Lankershim."

"We'll check that." I wrote it down with my government issue ballpoint. "Reverend, who else would have access to your boat?"

"Nobody, 'cept me 'n Nahan."

"That would be Wilton M. Nahan, your business manager. Does he sail the boat?"

"Naw, he just uses it to show off."

"Can you explain that, sir?"

"Well, he can't sail worth a damn, but he takes bidness clients down to the marina; entertains 'em on the boat."

Flipping to a new section of my notebook, I pretended to study a page. "We would be interested in knowing why a church might have business clients."

"Nahan does, not the church."

I produced a look both bored and skeptical. "Not according to our data. We've uncovered evidence of massive fraud, tax evasion, and illegal securities transactions. In fact, we were just about ready to move on this case."

Hammond looked increasingly angry. "It's not me; it's Nahan."

"Yes sir."

"I'm telling you, it was his game all along. Oh, I knew he was driving over the speed limit, but I thought it was little stuff. You know how it is with those figger-riggers; it's near automatic. Everybody does it. When I found out about this other stuff, I told him he was pushin' his luck some."

I kept it flat and tired. "When you found out."

"I would have blowed the whistle myself, but then how would that look for the church?"

"Was that the only reason you held back?"

"How do you mean?"

"We are aware of a certain pornographic film."

"*Hell* no! Nahan tried that on me. Must think I'm dumber'n a steer in a stockyard. I just laughed at him."

"He attempted to keep you quiet by threatening to expose your relationship with a pornographic actress, is that it?"

"Yeah; I could not believe my ears."

I covered some rapid thinking by scribbling busily in my notebook. Then: "Just a few more questions, sir. Do you know the present whereabouts of Lee Tolman?"

"I truly do not. Not for weeks."

"Concerning that Thursday afternoon, where was Mr. Nahan, do you know?"

"Like I said, I was tied up all afternoon."

"Tied up, sir. Could he sail your boat if he had to?"

"I showed him how to run the engine—to keep the batteries charged. He was always playing the stereo."

I nodded and wrote some more, then stared at him as if trying to make up my mind. Finally, "Sir, I don't believe it's necessary to continue at this time, but I'll have to ask you to keep yourself available."

Hammond relaxed visibly. "I want to clear this up as much as you do."

"And I would advise you to refrain from contacting Mr. Nahan." A meaningful look at my watch. "Our people are probably calling on him at about this time."

"Why sure."

I plodded back into the foyer, stowing pen and notebook. "Thank you for your cooperation, sir. You'll be hearing from us."

"You know where to find me."

My best Sergeant Friday look. "Yessir, we do."

I had to move fast now. Surprise and guilt had kept Hammond from looking too hard at my story. But now he'd have time to think about it and my cliché TV detective impression wouldn't stand much scrutiny.

I urged the Rabbit through the cool darkness down to Sunset, left to Crescent Heights, up again to Laurel Canyon.

My living room was dark except for the winking red eye on my telephone answering machine. I rewound the tape and played back the call.

"Stoney? Yeah, this is Gladys Dempal." She dropped briefly into cornball Slavic dialect: "Is fillink like sikret hagent. Listen, Stoney, it's five-fifty P.M. Pepe sat tight all afternoon. No calls; never left his office.

"Then about ten minutes ago, he made a call. A secretary said 'Mr. Nahan's office' and a man came on the line. Now I can't remember word for word, but I'll give you the gist. Pepe named you; said you'd found out about a certain film. The other man asked what you knew. Pepe said 'everything.' The man said that's bad. Pepe said it's worse: somebody named Peeper was dead.

"Dead? Hey, Stoney, this is serious stuff. You didn't tell me what I was getting into.

"Okay, the voice on the other end didn't react—I mean dead air for ten seconds. So Pepe said he was worried and did the other man know anything about this Peeper? More silence, then the other man sort of sighed. He told Pepe to stay at the studio and he would come over. Pepe asks what for and the other man says don't worry; just stay there 'til I come. Then he hangs—"

Click. Damn machine only records thirty-second messages. But Gladys did indeed deliver the gist.

It was after eight. Too late to catch them there.

I switched off the phone machine as I dug Lee's mother's business card out of my wallet. I called her beach house.

"Rachel Gershon."

"Ritchie, this is Stoney Winston, remember?"

"You're the jewel who does windows," delivered in a

three-scotch burr. I pictured Lee's mother propping up the counter in her kitchen, glass in one meaty hand, cigarette in the other. "You still looking for Beverly, kid?"

"That's why I called. I found her; but then I lost her again."

"She was here today."

Flush of relief: "Great!"

"She often checks in between saviors. Showed up on the bus this morning. Walked all the way down to the beach. Now she's off to Monterey."

"What for?"

"Salvation. Nirvana." Pause filled with what sounded like ice cubes clinking. "Touchies and feelies."

"What? . . ."

"Some commune or group or something."

"Had she been there before?"

"Well, she talked about 'going back.'"

That would explain Lee's cryptic remarks to Herbie. "Believe it or not, Ritchie, that might be the safest place for her."

"Good as any, until she wears it out and gets restless again. It never lasts."

"Okay, well, I promised to call you."

"Yeah."

"Good-bye, Ritchie."

So that's all there was to Lee's disappearance. The spirit having moved her, she had set out on the road to Damascus or Mecca or the Emerald City.

Or some damn place. Good luck, Lee, and good hunting. Bur remembering her puzzled green eyes, I doubted she'd have either.

Probably should call Denise and tell her where Lee was . . . my God! I never told her Lee was alive—or that I had the blackmail film. The last two days had moved so fast, I never thought to. I could do better than phone: I'd collect the film from my cutting room and present it to Denise gift-wrapped.

16

RATTLING THROUGH THE NIGHT DOWN TO DENISE'S studio to collect the original film. By now, I could probably make this run without steering. Just let the Rabbit have its head.

I was imagining Denise's face when I dropped the film in her lap and told her Lee was safe and sound. No more extortion and no threat to the studio sale. It felt good: Stoney Winston, mild-mannered director by day. . . .

I drove through the garish blaze on Hollywood Boulevard, past strolling adolescents and bag ladies and tourists gaping at the hookers.

Not so good about Peeper, though; remembering her chirpy energy and the innocence shining through her face paint.

I chuffed to a stop in the studio parking lot between a muscle bound Pontiac bearing the license plate PEPEDEL and a sedate Cadillac Seville. If Pepe was still inside, then the Seville might belong to Nahan. Stealth time.

I eased my key into the lobby door lock, wincing at the deadbolt's *clack*, then slipped in and shut the door gently. Dead silence except for the distant whoosh of passing cars. Blue-white wash from a single lit fluorescent in the hall. Up the stairs, keeping feet close to the wall to minimize creaking—a technique perfected for boyhood midnight snacks. I paused at the second floor corridor. To the left, a faint glow visible from around the corner near the row of cutting rooms. To the right, the closed door of Pepe's office, leaking light onto the faded carpet. Padding toward it, I checked the .38 in its hired holster.

Silence behind the door. Long, irresolute pause, then I
pulled out the pistol, turned the handle, and pushed the
door open.

I froze.

Pepe sprawled with one cheek mashed against the carpet in a puddle of clotting blood, staring at one outstretched
hand with empty, taxidermist's eyes. His lips were pulled
back from perfect cornrow teeth in a grin that looked no
phonier dead than alive.

Pushing against the door, I shut it to just short of latch-
ing. A quick survey confirmed that the office was empty.
Someone had ransacked it, opening files and strewing their
contents over the carpet, dumping drawers, pulling boxes
from the open closet. Pepe's pockets had been turned out;
his wallet and change lay on the floor beside him.

It didn't look professional—at least the way I'd seen it
staged in films: no slit upholstery, no dismantled pictures,
no turned-up rugs.

Covering my fingers with a handful of my jacket, I
pulled the door half open and eased back out into the hall. I
looked down toward the opposite corner, splashed by the
fluorescent overhead. Silence, then a faint metallic *clank*. A
pause. Another *clank*.

I paced very slowly toward the light, setting one foot
before the other as if trying to avoid touching the floor.
Stopping just short of the corner, I pasted myself to the wall
and looked around it.

The door to the film storeroom was open, edge toward
me, with a key ring still dangling from the deadbolt lock.
The room light was on and the tinny clanks were coming from inside. Back to the wall, I edged up to the storeroom and stopped in the shadow of the open door. The
room's occupant was still visible from my angle. Nothing to
do but take the plunge. Leveling the .38, I stepped into the
open doorway.

"Hello, Nahan."

He froze in the act of stripping tape from the edge of a
rusty film can. Scores of other cans were strewn about, lids

off, contents spilling everywhere. Endless snakes of film streamed off the metal shelves, corkscrewing downward into snarls hundreds of feet long. The floor was invisible under six inches of shiny flat spaghetti. Some of it was ancient nitrate stock so brittle that it had crumbled when it hit the floor.

Nahan glanced at the stumpy little revolver that lay on a shelf three feet from his hand. I grabbed it. Nahan looked at me blankly, then with mechanical deliberateness, finished opening the can he held. Flinching from the emerging stench, he dropped the can and a rain of gray-brown powder splashed his shoes.

"That nitrate film is dangerous. Besides, your dirty movie isn't here. I've got it." He glared. "And I just found Pepe. Did you kill him to get the film?"

Silence.

"Why did you kill Peeper?"

Nahan managed an imperious stare. "I don't have to speak to you."

No he didn't. Time for the most convincing performance I have ever given: I settled my face into the implacable calm of a wooden Indian and began speaking like a very reasonable child: "You think I'll call the police but I won't."

"What do you mean?"

"You killed Lee Tolman."

"That's absurd."

"She's gone."

Nahan shrugged, knowing as well as I did that he hadn't killed Lee.

I elaborated my grief-crazed role, keeping my voice unnaturally flat: "Lee would never have left without telling me. She loved me." I let my voice strangle and fail, then recover: "And I loved her too. And you killed her."

"I said—"

"You're going to get away with killing Peeper Martin. Her body's gone for good and I'm the only one who saw it. And I didn't recognize you in the dark. No body; no witness; no conviction."

Nahan considered this.

"I didn't see you kill Pepe either, and now I've grabbed your gun and wiped out your fingerprints."

Nahan's reaction showed he hadn't thought of this.

"People have tried to nail you for years and you've wiggled out every time. Every single time. I can't let that happen again—for Lee's sake."

"Wait—"

I rode over him in the same gentle monotone. "I don't care about Pepe and I don't care about Peeper but I do care about Lee. And I'm going to punish you for killing her because no one else will."

"You—"

"I'm going to shoot you and then I'm going to put the gun in your hand. You've already fired it, so the police will find powder traces on your hand. It will work very nicely."

"You won't do it."

Still insanely reasonable: "I have to. It's the only way to punish you—unless you tell me what you did with Lee. *They'll* convict you then."

"That's illogical."

"All right, we are going to walk back to Pepe's office and you're going to stand in his blood and I'm going to shoot you in the forehead." I paused, looking puzzled. "I think I better shoot you in the forehead because I'm not sure I can hit your heart with one shot. You see what I mean? Maybe it'll hit a rib or go right through or something."

"Listen!"

"Or maybe I should open your mouth and stick the gun in there and blow the back of your head off. Yes, that's a good idea. I think that's the way they usually do it."

I delivered this monologue in a relentlessly friendly voice, as if discussing ledger entries, and by the time I was through, Nahan's face was working.

"I did not kill your . . . Lee!"

"I think we better start now. Or I could kill you here and drag you." I pointed both pistols at him.

"Let's discuss this. How can I prove I did not kill the girl?"

"You killed Peeper."

Nahan clenched both hands in irritation. "That had nothing to do with—anything." Nahan actually looked embarrassed. "I had been . . . seeing Peeper. We met through Pepe. I took her to the boat because it was more private. I have a certain reputation, and she was not exactly . . ."

Keeping up my mind, mad delivery, "That's not an answer."

"When you told Peeper about the pornography, she was frightened. She telephoned me, insisted upon seeing me. I met her at the boat. She wanted to leave town and she wanted money to do it."

"Why?"

Nahan shrugged disgustedly. "She admitted that she and Pepe were using the film to extort money from the girl's mother—rather ineptly, I suspect. Peeper thought you were close to discovering them."

"But why did you kill her?"

"I don't customarily lose my temper, but I grew angry. Peeper and Pepe were jeopardizing other plans of mine."

"For the film?"

Nahan nodded. "When I spoke my mind, she grew loud and abusive. I didn't want the whole marina listening, so I slapped her—not hard. Her head hit the corner of some electronics box."

"The Loran receiver."

"I wouldn't know. But she was dead. It was the worst possible luck." Nahan sounded exasperated at Peeper's inconsiderateness in dying on him. "Then you appeared at the boat. There was no time to lock you out, so I concealed her in one of those narrow beds and hid in the front of the boat."

"And when I came below, you climbed out the forward hatch and locked me in. How did you manage to sail the boat?"

"I didn't. I only knew how to turn on the engine, so I drove the boat as if it were a car. I did well enough."

"You motored out into the shipping lanes and dumped her body."

"I put her in a sail bag with a pair of anchors and their chains. It worked satisfactorily." Again, Nahan's eerie focus on details, as if discussing an accounting procedure.

"How did you navigate?"

"I waited until daylight. The Pacific coast is hard to miss." Nahan actually smiled at his little joke.

"Who were those men you sent to kill me?"

"I was surprised at their ineptitude. They'd proved reliable on past occasions."

"Did they kill Lee?"

"I told you—".

"Why did you have her make that film? To use on Hammond?"

"She told you that? Yes, an ill-considered plan. But he was taking an unnecessary interest in things."

"Church finances."

"He was meddling in certain enterprises."

"Did you really think you could keep him in line with that tape?"

"I only required a few weeks. I hoped it would work that long."

"So you could finish draining the church and leave."

"In retrospect, it does seem inadequate."

"Why did you kill Pepe?"

Nahan clenched his hands again at an untidy world. "Another stupid accident. It was *his* gun. He waved it at me when I demanded the film." With a touch of pride: "I removed it from him without difficulty, but it discharged in the process. Quite unnecessary."

"Why did you want the film?"

"I prefer to be neat. The film was evidence."

"But Pepe made a tape copy to use on Mrs. Tolman. Didn't you realize that?"

"Another copy?" He looked blank momentarily, then sighed. "No." He shook his head several times, his face working. "No I did not. Another copy."

Keeping a careful watch on Nahan, I checked the door: the only lock was the deadbolt, on the corridor side.

"I'm going to leave you here while I call the police."

"I didn't kill Lee Tolman."

I dropped the crazy act abruptly: "I knew that, but I needed a threat to make you talk."

Nahan glared. "You never intended to kill me."

"A tempting thought, but no. You'll be all right in here until the police come. There's an air vent."

I shut the door on Nahan's furious face. I had to force it against the sea of film covering the floor and several brittle snarls escaped under the door and streamed out into the hallway. Still, I managed to push it shut and throw the deadbolt.

Then I started down toward Gladys' phone to call the law.

But first, back to Pepe's office to discard Nahan's gun. Going to be one unholy mess when the police arrive, and a lot of explaining to do.

I surveyed the disaster in Pepe's office. Plucking a Kleenex from a box on the desk, I wiped my prints off the gun and placed it on the bloody carpet. That would simplify my story for the law.

Then down the stairs to the first floor hall, which suddenly smelled of gasoline.

Gasoline?

17

DARK SPLOTCHES SOAKED THE CHEAP CARPET IN A TRAIL leading to the soundstage door. When I pulled the heavy stage door open, an immense whoosh of flames drove me back. The soundstage was engulfed. I tried to force the stage door closed to cut down the air draft but the heat was blasting through the doorway. Impossible. I raced down the corridor toward the lobby to call the fire department. I glanced back as I wrenched open the door: the flames had found the trail of gasoline on the carpet, which ignited like a wick. Abruptly, the sprinklers erupted and six pathetic piddles splashed the floor.

Into the dark lobby, fumbling the phone, dialing the operator to report the fire. Then, out of there before it spread.

Nahan! I'd locked him in the upstairs storeroom. I opened the lobby door again. Carpet blazing, wall paint bubbling and catching fire. I charged down the hall toward the staircase, shielding my head with my arms. The staircase carpet was shooting flames. No way up; back to the lobby.

Near Gladys' desk, a metal stand dispenser held a ten-gallon bottle of spring water. I heaved the bottle off the stand. Too heavy to lift over my head. Lying down, I wrestled the bottle onto my chest, tilting it over my wind-breaker until the water was half gone, and dumped the remainder over my head. Then soaking wet, I headed down the tunnel of roiling orange flames to the stairwell.

No good: stairwell was solid fire all the way to the second floor. White smoke billowed in the updraft; embers charred my clothes where the water missed. Back into the lobby again, eyes streaming, lungs stinging with smoke.

There was a fire escape in back; I'd used it before to get onto the roof. Must be fire doors opening on to it. I sped out the front door, through the parking lot, around to the rear of the building, and up the rusty iron staircase, heedless of feeble treads and shaking railings, to a door on the second floor landing.

Locked of course. I peered through the glass panel: flames engulfed the inside stairwell on the far side of the storage room where Nahan was trapped.

And I trapped him. I had to break in. The glass panel was reinforced with heavy wire mesh. I needed something to smash it.

Back down the rotten steps, jumping, stumbling, hands scraped by the rusty railing, to the back parking lot below. Trash bins! I flailed through coffee cups, papers, film trims, and boxes. Nothing heavy.

Wait: someone had smashed a concrete parking bumper, breaking off a foot-long piece. Hefting it—my God concrete's heavy—I staggered back up the stairs with my ingot-shaped weapon.

The fire had reached the second floor hallway: the carpet flaming, paint burning. Pressing the concrete chest-high like a weight lifter, I bashed the glass. It crazed but the wire mesh held. Again! Three strands of mesh snapped, opening an inch-wide hole. I drew back for another heave. The fire had reached the storeroom, inches away from the film looping out under the locked door.

The film! That old cellulose nitrate stock is gun powder. I was frozen by this thought; hypnotized by the searing yellow glare in the hallway.

One flame finger touched the film; the pile blazed instantly and flames rushed toward the door as if along a quick-match fuse. Under the door.

A long pause, then Nahan screamed and screamed. Even over the fire and through two doors, I could hear his agony. He was standing ankle-deep in loose film. The acetate stock would curl and melt but the nitrate film ignited like magnesium. Nahan was roasting to death.

He must have been pounding on the door, stamping on the flaming film, beating at his clothing. And still screaming, screaming. An eternity of anguished shrieks, then nothing but the roar of flames.

Shaky hands dropping the concrete to the iron landing; staggering down the groaning steps, shivering in my sopping jacket, breath whistling through my nose. Sirens keening in the distance.

The Rabbit! I didn't want to be here when the fire engines pulled in. Too much to do to hang around answering questions.

I pelted back to the front parking lot. The area was deserted. Smoke boiled up from the studio roof but there were no visible flames yet to attract a crowd. I jumped into the Rabbit; starter grinding; engine wheezing; firing; quick reverse; then I swung around and into the street.

I pulled over like any good citizen as the fire trucks screamed past me toward the studio.

I parked in the shadow of a closed Arco gas station and sat behind the wheel, willing my heart and breath to slow and my mind to erase the sounds of Nahan as he barbecued to death. I was half-retching at the smoke stench rising from my soggy jacket. I checked to see that the area was deserted and wobbled over to a public phone.

Denise picked up the receiver instantly: "Yes?"

"Denise, this is Stoney."

"Stoney!"

"I don't know what to say, Denise. I thought I had wonderful news. Lee is alive and well after all, and I found the film."

"Lee's alive? That *is* wonderful."

"But I'm afraid your studio's burning down."

"What?"

"Someone soaked it with gas and lit a match. It's going to be a total loss."

"Oh no!"

"Listen: I'm coming out to your house. I should be there in half an hour."

"You don't have to, Stoney."

"I owe you that much."

I hung up. Then soaking, filthy, singed and guilty of manslaughter, I aimed the failing Rabbit at Pasadena.

Groaning down the Hollywood Freeway toward the downtown oasis of lit skyscrapers, I wondered what the police would make of Denise's studio: one charred corpse in a ransacked storeroom. Another shot to death in his office, gun beside him on the floor—if there was any floor left. It would seem as if the lot had been torched to cover up the killings.

I swung through "the stack" and headed north on the Pasadena Freeway, the Rabbit engine noisily rehearsing a deathbed scene.

As for motive, Pepe and Nahan were both involved in a pornography operation. Plenty for the cops to chew on there. *Studio Victim of Gangland Arson*, etc.

And when Nahan's trail led back to the church, the scandal would put Hammond out of business faster than any porno tape.

Not a day too soon.

I roared down San Rafael Avenue in the creamy glow of the old-fashioned streetlights and turned into San Rafael Circle. Flying toward the turnaround at the bottom of the street, I screeched into a right turn, then accelerated up Denise's long driveway.

Suddenly a pair of double headlights swung toward me at the top of the drive and a car rushed forward. No chance to stop; I was doing thirty up the drive. Instead, I swerved hard left and floored it.

Right into the tree beside the driveway. The car's front end crumpled like a stomped-on beer can and the seat belt grabbed me an inch from the windscreen. Then the other car hit me broadside.

When the double crash had died away and I'd re-
gathered my senses, I forced the door open, got out, and
walked shakily around the Rabbit's remains. Lucky it was
the passenger side: the right door was pushed in two feet by
the massive nose of a red Cadillac Eldorado, from which the
figure of Harry Hummel was emerging in righteous wrath.

"Goddam son of a *bitch*! Look what you did to my
car!"

"Greetings, Harry."

"Winston, get your goddam piece of junk out of the
way. I'm in a hurry."

"Not any more."

"I'm not gonna play with you, shithead; move it!"

"How?"

"I don't care. I'll push you." He started for his car.

"Hummel!"

He jerked his door open, then stopped at the sight of
the .38 in my hand. "What? . . ."

"Calm down, Harry; there's no place to go."

"What's that thing for?"

"I want your cooperation and I'm too tired to beat it out
of you; so just reach in and get your car keys."

"You can't—"

Stepping forward, I slammed the gun barrel into his
ribs as hard as I could. "Keys!"

"All *right*, jeez!" He pulled them out of the ignition.

"Unlock your trunk."

"Hey!"

Another stab with the gun barrel. "Harry, don't push
your luck."

Reluctantly, he found the key, unlocked the trunk, and
raised the lid. The trunk was filled with gas cans. I hefted
one: empty.

"Let's go see Denise."

Hummel opened his mouth, but I slammed the trunk
lid and gestured with the gun. He closed his mouth and
turned toward the house. I followed with the gas can.

"Listen, Stoney: about the cans. I always carry them. Insurance, right?"

"Yeah, fire insurance. Ring the bell."

He did. "I was gonna talk to you about something. You been doing all the work on our productions and I thought maybe you oughta be a partner."

"You'll have to let me sign the checks."

"We can work that out."

"Because you'll have trouble running the company from your cell."

Denise opened the door, dressed in a tartan skirt and soft blouse, looking anxious. "What was all that noise?"

"Harry sent my Rabbit to the great Hutch in the sky. It's totaled." Denise peered around us, down the drive. "He also wants to say good-bye before he goes to jail for arson." I raised the gas can for inspection.

Denise looked uncertainly from the can to Hummel to me. "I guess you better come in."

18

DENISE LED THE WAY TO THE FAMILY ROOM: ROUND MAPLE
table, Amish-design wallpaper, hardwood railing high on
the wall displaying commemorative plates ordered in series
by mail. An overscale grandfather clock parodied Big Ben as
I dropped onto a chair, then it chimed eleven. I suddenly
realized how wretched I felt: reeking, dank, and so tired
that my thighs were trembling under the table.

Denise sat opposite with her hands on the flowery
cloth, fingers laced together. Hummel reversed a chair and
sat with his chin just above its ladder back. We faced one
another like poker players under the plastic Tiffany chan-
delier.

I explained how and why Nahan talked Lee into faking
the film. But his scheme to blackmail Hammond was so
farfetched that the preacher just laughed at it.

I recounted how Pepe got the bright idea to recycle the
film by using it to extort money from Denise. But he and
Peeper were so inept that they never progressed past a
phone call and a melodramatic letter.

I repeated Nahan's story of how he'd killed Peeper
completely by accident when she came to Hammond's boat
to ask for money.

All unrelated events, juxtaposed by chance to form a
plausible but meaningless design. It was as if two elephants
were standing back to back. Blind Winston felt their parts
and announced: "An elephant has four hind legs." Delbert
was right after all: it's not cause and effect; it's one damn
thing after another.

Denise cleared her throat. "I'm sorry for the other girl,
but it's wonderful that Lee's all right." She started to rise.
"Well, I'm glad it's all cleared up."

"Sit down, Denise. I told you on the phone that your studio was burning down."

Hummel looked at her, but she stared straight at me.

I continued, "But then, you already knew that, since you sent Harry to set fire to it."

"Oh, no . . ."

"I made the mistake of phoning you to say I was coming here. When Hummel showed up ahead of me, you told him to disappear fast. Unfortunately, my late Rabbit was blocking his exit. His trunk was full of empty gas cans."

Hummel aimed sincere blue eyes. "Just insurance, like I said."

"I know why you burned it. Your studio was unsalable: too old to fix up and too expensive to pull down. But if you burned it past repair, you could use some of the insurance money to clear the lot. You'd have thousands left over, plus two acres of prime commercial real estate in the middle of Hollywood. Correct?"

Hummel was growing nervous. "Yeah, but that's got nothin' to do with me."

"Perish the thought, Harry. Denise, whose idea was this?"

She looked at Hummel.

"What's he get out of it?"

"A percentage of the insurance."

"Don't count on it. When your lot cools down, the firemen are going to find two corpses in the rubble."

"What?"

"And Harry, you killed one of them."

"Hey, Jesus!"

"Nahan shot Pepe dead in his office. When I discovered him, I got Nahan's gun and locked him in the film storeroom. Before I could get back to let him out, Harry's little fire burned him up."

"My God!"

"It'll be a long time before the police sort that one out, and longer still before the insurance company decides what to do—if anything."

Denise's voice was alarmed: "What do you mean, *if anything?*"

I studied her plump, anxious face, floating in the cruel downlight from the Tiffany lamp. She looked her age and then some.

"It may take years before the whole thing's settled. What'll you live on in the meantime?" Denise looked puzzled. "You said that studio was your sole source of income, correct?" A nod. "No one will pay you to rent a burnt-out shell, Denise. Where will you get money?"

"Harry?" Her mastermind just shrugged. "Harry, where *will* I?" Hummel had the grace to look embarrassed. "You never thought of that; you didn't tell me."

"And you let Hummel do your thinking for you."

"I didn't deserve this!"

"Before turning into a puddle of self-pity, you may want to reflect that you killed three people."

"*I* didn't!"

"You turned me loose on Peeper and Pepe. Peeper went to Nahan because I scared her. Pepe called Nahan because I scared *him*. Nahan died too, because you burned down your studio for the insurance."

"You'll get twelve hundred dollars out of it."

"I wouldn't touch it. But you do owe me something: the truth about why you hired me."

Denise studied her perfect fingernails. "Well, it was a reason for not calling the police about the blackmail. You know that letter I showed you, with the threat and all?" I nodded. "You see, it didn't come a couple days ago, it arrived two weeks back, along with the tape."

"Even before the first phone call?"

"Yes, so we had this idea—Harry and I."

Hummel began: "It wasn't *my* . . ."

"We'd . . . get rid of the studio and *then* show the letter to the police. They'd think arson was the threat the letter talked about."

"Sort of farfetched. Where did I come in?"

"We needed time to . . . get ready, you know, so I—couldn't go to the police right away. I had to have a reason to hold off. You were it."

"How?"

"Our story was I was afraid of scandal. So instead of telling the police right away, I hired somebody."

"And you hoped an amateur like me wouldn't really find anything." I stared up into the light, sighing. "You weren't connected to anything, either. You're a third pair of hind legs."

"Hm?"

"On Winston's composite elephant. I thought the studio was part of a pattern, but it was just Laurel and Hardy playing criminals." I forced myself to stand. "Time to call the police, Harry."

"Hey, wait a minute!"

"We have to report an auto accident, remember? And you might want to get the other gas cans out of your trunk."

Hummel's relief was pathetic to behold. "Yeah, okay." He hustled out.

I looked at Denise. "Was it Hummel's idea?"

"Well, yes, I guess it was. Sure."

"And you just took his advice." As I watched Denise, her plump allure evaporated, revealing the faded, empty pom-pom girl, face puckered by self-pity. "You'll have to sell this house to raise cash."

"What!"

"Get a little place in Burbank or somewhere. Use the rest to live on until you find work."

"What could I work at?"

"Beats me. Wait tables. Clerk at Sears."

"I couldn't do that."

"Surprising what you can do if you need the money. But then, you know that." No reaction. Nothing broke her shell of selfishness—certainly nothing *I* could say. "Goodbye, Denise."

*   *   *

Sinking into the glove-leather passenger seat of Hummel's
Eldorado, which had sustained only cosmetic damage in
the course of dismantling the Rabbit.

"Nice of you to drive me home, Harry."

"Stupid cops asked a million questions. Why was I
going so fast? Why didn't I see you? Jeez."

"Always be polite to the law."

"Did you mean it: not telling them about the fire?"

"That's negotiable."

"Huh?"

"You destroyed my car, so it's only fair that you replace
it."

"I got insurance."

"Uh-huh, and what's Blue Book on a '75 Rabbit? A de-
cent used car will cost six times that much."

"Well that's the breaks."

"*Eight* times that much. Want to try for ten?"

"Is this like blackmail?"

"Not yet, but the idea has a certain crude justice."

"What?"

"Never mind." I was suddenly too disgusted to bother.
"Tomorrow, you are going to buy me a used Volkswagen." I
glanced at the digital dashboard clock. "I mean today. Pick
me up at noon."

"We'll talk about it."

"Or fifteen minutes later, I call the police."

"All *right*. Shit!"

"Always a pleasure doing business with you."

19

LOUNGING IN A CHAISE ON SALLY'S DECK, I WATCHED THE
autumn sun sink through bright amber air toward the Pacific, visible twenty miles away. Still eighty degrees out
here, but dropping fast. "Hard to believe it's fall again."

Sally sat up on her tanning mat, removing plastic eye
cups. "How can you tell?"

"I admit it took me five years in L.A. to learn we had
seasons and ten more to tell them apart. Aren't you getting
cold?"

"Not yet." She studied me. "Still bothered?"

"I wish it were a movie, without real pain and death."

"If only."

"With a tidy movie plot. At the end of the film, I get
everyone together in the library. First I trace an elegant
chain of cause and effect. Then I run through a long list of
suspects, discarding each for impeccable reasons, until my
brilliant reasoning has found the only possible villain."

Sally rose and joined me at the rail.

"Cut to exterior as police car drives up, roll end credits
over the shot, fade out. Exeunt satisfied moviegoers. Why
isn't life like that? Why is harmless Pooper dead?"

"Death frightens you."

"Well sure; and chaos. Patterns comfort me."

She smiled fondly. "I know."

"So I see them where they don't exist."

"Not always." She wrapped an arm around my waist.
"Sometimes, you imagine them so hard you make them
happen." She flashed her sardonic grin. "Believe me."

Hoping I read her right, I almost pursued the topic.
No, give her world enough and time. Instead, I broke the
moment: "Hmp. Stay warm now; let's go in."

179

As we started around the side deck, Sally glanced down at the gleaming silver insect crouched in the driveway below. "Hey, is *that* your new car?"

"Yup: a Beetle convertible—the last model year. Twenty thousand miles; mint condition; sport suspension; Recaro seats—the lot."

"Hummel must of bled."

"Today, he finally pushed me too far: I suggested a Ford or something and he blew his stack: cursed me up and down, announced that I'd never work in this town again, and wound up by screaming, 'a bleeping used VW is what you said and a bleeping used VW is all you get!'"

Sally chortled at my Hummel-style delivery.

I smiled down at the sparkling car. "So when we reached the dealer, I murmured 'gas can' in Harry's shell-like ear and picked a used VW: that one."

Sally's grin faded into a pensive look. "You can't keep it, you know."

"For two weeks' work and a Rabbit? It's a fair trade. Call it poetic justice."

"But not *real* justice." Then doubtfully: "You should tell the police."

"What would I say?"

"That Peeper and Pepe blackmailed Denise. That Nahan killed them both. That Nahan tried to blackmail the preacher. That Hummel and Denise committed arson. That . . ." Sally trailed off as the difficulties dawned on her.

"Uh-huh, they don't have Peeper's body—or her killer. Just my word for it, and of course, I somehow neglected to report it when I found her. So careless of me, officer. What *could* I have been thinking?"

"There is the film."

"The film is burnt and the blackmailers are dead. You think Hammond's going to come forward—or Denise?"

Sally's voice lacked conviction: "It still doesn't seem . . . right."

"They're all dead. Isn't that enough?"

"Not Denise and Hummel."

"Denise lost half a million dollars. And Harry's out of business."

"Why?"

"The cola spots. He had to put up a performance bond to get the job."

"That's unusual, isn't it?"

"Not with Hummel's track record. But he never did get a bond—just bluffed it through. Now his film and soundtrack are ashes in my cutting room and there's no way he can deliver. I even had the original—to take to the negative cutter."

"The client will be peeved."

"At least breach of contract—maybe fraud. And the word gets around the agencies. Anyone can have bad luck, but Hummel's screwed them once too often."

Sally sighed and nodded. "Okay, but if you keep that car, you're no different from Hummel."

"And how am I supposed to get from A to B?" Irritated, I stomped over to the railing and flailed an arm at the view beyond. "This is L.A., remember?"

Sally saw I was angry because I didn't like what I knew I had to do. She smiled and nodded.

"Hey! I could ride the bus—they come by at least once a week."

Sally looked at me.

"Or a skateboard."

Silence.

I pulled in a long breath full of dusty autumn smells. "I'll give it back to him."

Sally frowned. "No, Hummel deserves what he got— and then some. Give it to charity."

"The home for indigent directors. Little enlightened self-interest."

"Or self-pity." She wrapped an arm around my waist.

"True. You're right."

"At least, you'll never work for Hummel again."

"Now that's the best promise you could make me."

Well, maybe *second* best.

ABOUT THE AUTHOR

Taught to write and make films by Harvard and UCLA, respectively, JIM STINSON is remembered for his contributions to such seminal works as "The Mineral Composition of Granite" and "Electrical Hazards in the Coronary Care Unit," as well as "Count Yorga, Vampire," and four features that were never released. Pursuing a lifelong interest in solvency, he then became an instructional designer and writer of business training programs. When not writing fiction and criticism, he composes computer software manuals, which he claims are not state-of-the-art because the state of the art is wretched. He lives with his wife and two teen-age children in Pasadena, California, where his presence is largely undetected.